C0-APG-374

LACKBEARD

CODY B. STEWART AND ADAM ROCKE

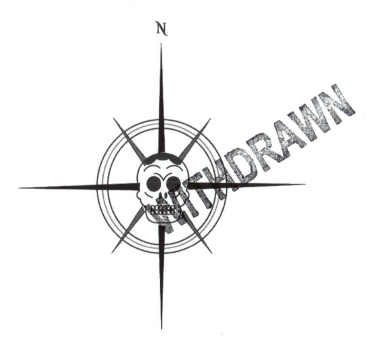

3 1336 10596 9944

COMMON DEER PRESS

WWW.COMMONDEERPRESS.COM

Published by Common Deer Press Incorporated.

Copyright © 2018 Cody B. Stewart and Adam Rocke

All rights reserved under International and Pan-American Copyright Conventions. No part of this book may be reproduced in any form or by any electronic or mechanical means, including information storage and retrieval systems, without permission in writing from the publisher, except by a reviewer, who may quote brief passages in a review.

Published in 2018 by Common Deer Press
3203-1 Scott St.
Toronto, ON
M5V 1A1

This book is a work of fiction. Names, characters, places, and incidents are either the product of the author's imagination or are used fictitiously.

Library of Congress Cataloging-in-Publication Data
Stewart, Cody B.; Rocke, Adam.—First edition.
Lackbeard / Cody B. Stewart and Adam Rocke
ISBN 978-1-988761-24-4 (print)
ISBN 978-1-988761-25-1 (e-book)

Cover Image: © Tim Zeltner i2i art
Book Design: Ellie Sipila

Printed in Canada

WWW.COMMONDEERPRESS.COM

Ox 1-19 √ 3-19

WITHDRAWN

LACKBEARD

For Sammi and Taylor, I will forever cherish all our adventures together.

-AR

For Finn. Haul on the Bowlin.

-CBS

There comes a time in every rightly constructed boy's life when he has a raging urge to go somewhere and dig for hidden treasure.

— Mark Twain

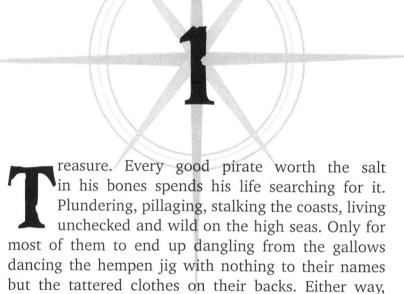

Treasure. Every good pirate worth the salt in his bones spends his life searching for it. Plundering, pillaging, stalking the coasts, living unchecked and wild on the high seas. Only for most of them to end up dangling from the gallows dancing the hempen jig with nothing to their names but the tattered clothes on their backs. Either way, it's a sad end to a life meant for nonstop adventure, unimaginable riches, and boundless freedom.

But not Carter Humbolt. He'd have his freedom if he had to cut through all of St. Augustine to get it.

Or he'd just sneak out. Yeah, probably just sneak out.

And he'd have his treasure, too—even if he had to level the St. Augustine Pirate and Treasure Museum to get it.

Or he could just pick the lock. Yeah, probably just do that.

Because Carter was the scourge of Castillo Drive! The sea-faring scoundrel of St. John's County! A shadow in the dead of night! The most fearsome—

"Carter!"

The sharp whisper shook Carter from his fantasy

and dropped him back into the larceny at hand. Brad Humbolt, reluctant buccaneer and first mate of naysaying, breathed down his little brother's neck. "This is a terrible idea. I mean a *really* terrible idea. I definitely should not have agreed to this."

"Sturdy yer mainsail, jelly bones," Carter grumbled in his gruffest pirate voice. He didn't take his eyes off the keypad, its blinking lights like the stars that guided his ship. Or would if he had a ship.

"I have no idea what you just said," Brad growled, stooping down close to Carter's ear, "but I think I might pound you for it anyway—if we don't end up in jail."

Carter pulled his skull and crossbones hood up over his headlamp. He flicked it on and drenched the keypad in red light. He cracked his knuckles. "It'll be open seas and fair winds for us, laddy."

Brad scoffed as he paced behind Carter. Brad was sixteen, athletic, and would fit in on any high school sports team, playing any position. Cheerleaders would swoon. Parents would wish their kids were more like him. The coach would call him in to win the game...

Or in another life he would, anyway. But in this life, he just paced and watched as his twelve-year-old brother, the perpetual mischief-maker, sized up a high-tech alarm's digital keypad, preparing to break and enter.

"Can the pirate stuff," Brad said. "Just hurry up. There are no fair winds in prison. Just broken wind and other clouds of man stink."

"C'mon," came a soft voice from around the corner. "Where's your sense of adventure?" Darla Roberts appeared as if she were out for a casual stroll. She was casual in many senses of the word—never tried to impress anyone, never cared what anyone thought—but was always down for some excitement.

Carter could practically hear Brad's heart jump.

"Hiding behind my sense of self-preservation," Brad answered. "I wouldn't do very well in prison."

"No, you're much too pretty," Darla said with a chuckle.

"And he's a nervous pooper," Carter added.

Brad choked.

Before his brother could strangle him, Carter unzipped his backpack and said, "Now, everyone be quiet. I need to concentrate."

To anyone else, the contents of his bag would have seemed a hodgepodge collection of worthless junk. To Carter, it was an adventurer's toolkit—a pirate's war chest. He laid out everything he would need—rubber dish gloves, a corroded lawn mower battery, a pair of knitting needles, and some strands of wire with alligator clips.

Carter slipped on the rubber gloves because adventure without the proper safety precautions is just reckless. Then he attached the alligator clips to the battery leads and tied the wire from the clips to the knitting needles. He touched the ends of the needles and watched as sparks danced like fireflies through the air.

"Oh, man," Brad grumbled. "You're totally gonna electrocute yourself."

Darla shushed him.

In another life, Carter Humbolt would have been a promising young scholar, a future engineer, a pioneer in robotics. In this life, however, he was a budding criminal, breaking into museums with knitting needles.

He poked at the keypad, inserted the needles into the small openings in the side. A quick stream of sparks shot out followed by a small plume of black smoke and the smell of burning plastic.

"Avast, me hardies," Carter said through a wide smile. "The gateway is open."

Brad shook his head. "I think something might be seriously wrong with you. Like, maybe Mom dropped you on your head or something as a baby."

Carter's expression turned sour and his smile slid off his face. He packed it away in his bag with his supplies. "Yeah, well, I wouldn't know about that."

Darla smacked Brad on the shoulder and gave him a cross look before following Carter through the now unlocked door.

Carter pushed his brother's comment to the back of his mind and pulled something else forward to replace it. All his favorite stories from the Golden Age of Piracy—Blackbeard, Calico Jack, Black Bart. Legendary brigands of the sea. He pulled the strings on his hoodie, tightening the skull and crossbones around his head, and became one of them.

He stepped into the unlit hallways. The shadows were his home. The darkness was his kin. He was the nightmare of—

"Crap!" Carter whisper-shouted. He put his arms out, stopping Brad and Darla behind him.

Brad spun around like a cat chasing its tail. "What? Who? Where?"

Darla choked back a laugh.

"There," Carter said, pointing at a metal box on the wall. "Countermeasures."

Brad squinted into the dark. "I don't see anything."

"Ye don't see the kraken 'til it strikes. That don't mean it's not lurking below." Carter reached into his bag of mayhem again and removed a plastic bottle of baby powder. "And you should probably eat more carrots. Your night vision is crapola."

"You should probably start seeing a shrink," Brad said. "I think you've lost it."

Carter squeezed the bottle of baby powder, and a mist of white puffed into the air. As the tiny particles fell, there showed a crisscrossing pattern of infrared beams. He shot Brad a self-satisfied smile. "There's a fine line between madness and genius."

Brad shoved his little brother aside and stepped past him. "Jury's still out as to which side you're standing on."

I walk a fine line between the two, Carter wanted to reply, but he kept his mouth shut.

The three of them skulked through the dark hallways, lit only occasionally by the dim neon of exit signs. None dared speak. None dared admit how nervous they were.

"Anyone else think a zombie is going to pop out around every corner?" Silence. "No? Just me?"

They passed by the gift shop. A vague memory crawled into Carter's head. It was hazy, like he was seeing it through a thick fog. A woman with long black hair carrying him. Where were they? A store? The beach? The smell of saltwater wafted on the air.

The memory continued…

He remembered feeling safe in her arms.

Someone tugged on his leg. Looking down, he saw the face of his brother. It was a bit pudgy. Brad couldn't have been more than eight.

"What about this?" little Brad said, holding up a small teddy bear that wore an eye patch and skull and crossbones bandana.

"Yes," the woman said. "I think Carter would like that very much." Then her voice dropped, became gruff. "Yer brother's got a pirate's soul."

Carter felt a tug on his arm, snapping him back to the task at hand.

"Come on," Darla said. "It's this way."

They rounded the corner and soon came to a wooden door. It looked out of place against the cold tile and metal of the rest of the museum. It looked warm, inviting, unique. It looked like part of a ship.

They exchanged glances. Excitement, curiosity, a little fear (Brad!). And then they opened it.

A gust of wind must have blown through an open window. No, that was just Carter gasping, sucking in the wonder of the room. Display cases lined the walls, each filled with piratical objects. Flintlock pistols, a cat-o'-nine-tails, a cutlass. Blunderbusses and spyglasses. An actual peg leg. Everything Carter needed to transform himself, to escape this life and build the one where he could be anything he dreamed of.

Well, almost everything he needed.

He peeled his eyes away from a hook hand and set to searching through cabinets and stacks of papers for that one last thing.

The one thing he had come here for.

"Oh. My. God." Darla's voice echoed from the far side of the room. She pressed her hands to a large display case. Brad shined his flashlight on the sign mounted above it.

TREASURE ROOM

"I found it," she said dreamily. She traced the glass with her finger, outlining the piles of gold and silver coins, the gem-encrusted scepter, the crown beset with shimmering gemstones on the other side. "We can leave. Live anywhere. On an island somewhere. Heck, we can *buy* an island."

"That's not what we're looking for," Carter snapped.

"Wait, what?" Darla said. "We broke in here to *not* steal the giant pile of treasure?"

"That stuff's traceable," Carter said. "As soon as we fenced it, we'd get busted. Haven't you seen any cop show ever? The treasure I'm after is much more—"

Before Carter could finish, the sound of a closing door echoed from the dark.

"Zombies!" Brad shrieked. "We're outta here."

"Not yet, I haven't found it."

"Doesn't matter," Brad said. "We need to leave *right now*. We can't spend any treasure in prison."

"Just one more minute," Carter argued. "It's gotta be around here somewhere." But before the sentence fully left his mouth, Brad had pulled him out of the room.

They ran through the dark corridors, not even hesitating at corners to check for walking dead. They moved like ships with the wind in their sails. Like the very gods of the sea were pushing them forward. Like they were—

They burst through the door they'd come in through and slid to a halt, blinded by bright lights. Carter squinted through the pain. Red and blue lights flashed behind the men. The men with the flashlights. The men with the guns pointing straight at them.

The back seat of the police cruiser smelled like wet, old man. Like a wet, old man vomited up another wet, old man, and then the two of them fell asleep on a pile of half-digested cheese puffs.

"I knew it," Brad said. "I knew this would happen. These kinds of things *always* happen."

"Uh, I don't think this has ever happened to us before," Carter said.

"You know what I mean," Brad snapped. His voice boomed inside the car.

Carter forgot how intimidating his brother could be when he got mad. He was suddenly very grateful that Darla was sitting between them.

"These crazy ideas of yours," Brad continued. "They always land us in trouble. It's like you sit up at night, planning out the most efficient way of screwing up my life, and then, for some reason, I go along with them." He turned away from Carter, stared at the bustling police officers outside. "Maybe *I'm* the crazy one."

Carter bit down until his jaw ached. "Sorry I screwed up your life," he said through gritted teeth.

The cruiser felt like a submarine, buckling under the pressure of silence. And it had sprung a leak.

"Well," Darla said, trying to keep her head above water. "This was fun."

Carter's door swung open suddenly and the silence spilled out onto the street, saving them all from drowning in it.

"Out," said the police officer.

One by one, they climbed out of the car. Brad stuck his hands out in front of him, palms up. "I'm ready. Take me away. You'll charge me as a minor, right? I'm only sixteen. This is my first offense. And I'm a nervous pooper."

The officer stared at Brad a moment, until a fancy black car rolled up, and an intense-looking older man, maybe sixty, with cropped gray hair stepped out.

"Appreciate the call," the older man said as he shook the cop's hand.

"Not a problem, Mr. Croce. I'm sorry to bother you at this hour."

Carter's heart jumped at the mention of the man's name.

"How'd they get in?" Mr. Croce asked.

"Shorted the alarm on the back door," the cop said, holding up Carter's knitting needles and lawnmower battery burglar's tools, more than a little impressed. "If they hadn't tripped the silent, we might not have caught them."

"Silent alarm," Carter cursed as he slapped his forehead. "Rookie mistake."

Pat Croce stepped in front of Carter and looked down at him, studying him. "This was you?"

The lump in Carter's throat nearly choked him. "Yes, sir."

Mr. Croce studied him some more, cocking an eyebrow and barely suppressing a smile when he noticed the skull and crossbones on Carter's hoodie.

The police officer produced a hardbound book. "This was all we found on them."

Mr. Croce took it, and his eyebrow raised even higher, almost crawling right over the top of his head. "You rigged up a way to short out the alarm on the backdoor, snuck past a laser grid—just to steal my book?"

Carter stared at the title. *The Pirate Handbook* by Pat Croce.

"You can get this in any bookstore," Mr. Croce said. "You do know there's piles of treasure in there, right?"

"That's what I said," Darla added.

Carter's voice dropped. He took on the rusty, jagged edge of a well-used cutlass. "A real pirate takes what he pleases."

Croce fought back another smile.

The familiar squeal of a loose fan belt drew the attention from Carter. A white van pocked with spots of rust raced up the street and screeched to a halt behind the line of police cruisers. The writing on the side of it was peeling but still visible: *St. John's County Children's Orphanage.*

Jane Roberts, the director of the orphanage, slammed the van door and marched past the police officers who were trying to talk to her, self-righteous in her stride. "Where are they?" she demanded. "I'll chain them to their beds. I'll string them up by their toenails. I'll…" Her voice trailed off as she seemed to remember the abundance of law enforcement officials surrounding her. "Discipline them accordingly, in a manner that is both firm and loving."

Mr. Croce looked down at Carter. He no longer had the stern look of a plundered merchant, but the understanding of a fellow plunderer. He took a pen from his pocket and wrote something on the inside cover of the book, before handing it back to Carter.

Carter returned a face full of confusion, and continued to stare at Mr. Croce's back as he walked away.

"I'm not pressing charges," Mr. Croce said to the officer as he passed.

The cop seemed as confused as Carter.

"These kids have it bad enough as it is," Croce added.

Ms. Roberts marched front and center to the kids. "For years, I've busted my butt so you two could stay together," she growled, first sticking her finger in Brad's face, then Carter's. She met each of them with a glare that could make plastic flowers wilt. "And this is how you repay me? Burglary?"

"We didn't actually steal anything," Carter said. "Well, I guess I did, technically, but then Mr. Croce gave it to me, so in the end—"

Brad clapped his hand over Carter's mouth. "I'm sorry, Ms. Roberts. This was my fault. It won't happen again."

"You're right it won't!" Ms. Roberts straightened. A smile snaked its way across her forty-year-old face, crawling through the wrinkles she so often tried to hide. "Because I found a home for the little brat on the other side of the country." She leaned in close to Brad. He tried not to wince at the stink of cigarettes on her breath. "And I've found a place that'll make something out of your worthless butt. Valley Forge Military Academy. Heard of it?"

"Mom, you can't—" Darla began, but was silenced by a fierce look from her mother.

"Oh yes I can, and oh yes I will. I'll fill you in on your punishment later."

Ms. Roberts pulled Carter by the wrist toward the van. He felt like a wet blanket being dragged behind her.

The van door slid shut like the iron door of a prison cell. Brad was wrong. Prison would have been better.

3

It was the only room Carter had ever known, the small, barely-bigger-than-a-closet room at the orphanage that he'd shared with his brother for as long as he could remember. Two cots pressed against opposite walls. A small desk between them. He liked to imagine it as his quarters below deck of his pirate schooner. It may have been cramped, but what did that matter when the wide-open sea was just on the opposite side of his wall?

If only.

The room contained little, but what did he need that he could not take from the world out there? After all, you couldn't shove adventure into one tiny room.

Dreams aside, a tiny room is all it was. His cot was an uncomfortable length of cloth pulled over rusty springs that squealed with the tiniest movement. And the nothing he had in there was the same nothing that he had out there. The same nothing that he'd always had. The same nothing he would always have.

At least, if he allowed it to be that way.

Carter opened the book again, reading Mr. Croce's inscription for the hundredth time.

EMBRACE YOUR PIRATE SOUL, BUT NEVER AT MY EXPENSE.
~PAT CROCE

The flash of foggy memory played in his head again. "Yer brother's got a pirate's soul," she said. His mother. So long ago he wondered if it had happened at all.

Then he remembered what else he'd taken from the museum. What the police *hadn't* found.

Darla walked into the room without knocking. Her face was red like she'd been crying. Or maybe yelling. Probably yelling. "I can't believe my mom. She's such a raging…" She growled instead of finishing the sentence.

Brad lay on his cot, tossing his football in the air. "It's not her fault. She gave us plenty of chances. Really, you only need one chance to *not* break into a museum full of priceless artifacts. And we blew it." He caught his ball and turned to Carter. "I hope your stupid book was worth it. Now they're shipping me off to war."

Carter traced his finger along the inscription one more time before closing the book. "Actually, it was. You might want to look away," he then said to Darla.

Before she could react, he shoved his hand down his pants.

"Inappropriate," she shouted as she shielded her eyes. "It may be time for you to have *that talk* with your brother," she said to Brad.

"Eureka," Carter said as he removed his hand from his pants, holding a small wooden box, covered in symbols that looked like part of a forgotten language.

"What is that?" Darla said.

"A treasure chest," Carter answered with a smile.

"Looks like a pencil case," Brad said. "So I'm being

shipped off to war not just for a book, but so you can keep your pencils safe."

"Who even uses pencils?" Carter put his ear to the box. He ran his fingers along the length of it, hoping to hear it answer his unasked questions. His right index finger caught on something—the tiny pedestal foot on the bottom. It turned slightly with the pressure of his finger. He pressed it, and it moved more. He turned it in a full circle.

"Make that a *broken* pencil case," Brad added. "I'll need a better story to tell my brothers-in-arms when we're in the foxhole. Maybe I'll them I joined the army because I needed money to fix my brother's brain."

Ignoring his brother's whining, Carter scanned the books on his shelf, the only possessions he had in this world. Granted, they were all ratty and dog-eared. Some even had pages missing. But they were *his*. And all were pirate-related, of course. Biographies on legendary pirates. History books. Fictional adventure stories. Everything a boy needed to build a fantasy world of plunder and the wide-open seas. His finger landed on the one he needed—an index of pirate treasures and antiquities, objects used by the sea-faring legends themselves.

He opened to a page he'd previously marked, its corner folded over so many times it nearly fell off. He dropped the book on the desk for Brad and Darla to see. "Still think it's a pencil case?"

Darla sucked in a breath as she looked at a picture of the exact object Carter held in his hand. "No way."

Brad hopped off his bed. "Okay, so you actually took something of value. I don't know why you thought this would make me feel better."

"This is a four-lock box," Carter said as he read the passage in the book. "Made to hold something of great value." Suddenly, the rotating piece clicked.

The room went quiet.

Even Brad's eyes were glued to the thing now.

Carter moved his fingers up the box to another rotating piece. He turned it and *click*. Two more pieces. Two more clicks.

None of them were even breathing at that point.

The bottom panel of the box popped open. Carter's mind went blank. He felt like he should be thinking something. Imagining all the wonders that lay inside this artifact. All the amazing things he would do with it. But there was nothing.

Not until his fingers reached inside the box and brushed against that ancient scrap of vellum. He slid it out, and Darla's jaw dropped open.

"Don't even tell me," she said.

Brad stood upright for the first time since the cops stuffed him in the back of the cruiser. "You've gotta be kidding me."

The crinkling sound, like autumn leaves crunching underfoot as Carter unrolled the vellum was like a symphony in his ears. He imagined. He'd never heard a symphony. His heart stopped, froze, turned to a solid chunk of gold in his chest.

There, on the old paper, was a map, hand-drawn in dark crimson ink. A compass rose sat in the bottom left corner. Cracks ran through the paper. There were small blobs of ink in the lines where the hand drawing it had paused for a moment. Words were misspelled. Nothing was to scale.

It was perfect.

Darla extended her hand.

"Careful," Carter said, handing it over. "It's old."

"How old?" Brad asked.

Carter couldn't help but smile. He could barely speak without breaking out into laughter. His eyes filled with tears. "Golden Age of Piracy old. Over three hundred years."

Darla pointed to a spot on the map. "There's seriously an 'X' on here. Marking an actual spot."

"Not just any old X, but a German cross X," Carter corrected.

"What's the difference?"

Carter's smile grew even wider, if that were possible. "As everyone knows, an X shows where treasure is buried. But a German cross X..." Carter sighed. "Those were reserved for *great* treasure."

"How great?"

"Huge freakin' piles of pirate plunder."

Darla's awed expression exploded into one of pure glee. She jumped up and down, laughed, squealed, and then ran out of the room.

Carter and Brad stared after her, frozen like awkward, gawking statues.

"Did she just steal my map?" Carter asked in disbelief.

"Yup," Brad answered. "Welcome to the world of piracy."

They breathed a collective sigh of relief when Darla burst back into the room a moment later.

She held up her old, scuffed, and scratched iPad for them to see. "What do you see?" The boys looked for a moment, and then she held the map up next to it.

"Shiver me timbers," Carter said. "They be twins."

The shapes on both matched. The landmarks, the

positioning of the water. No question about it, they were the same.

"Where?" Brad said.

Darla tapped the screen, zooming out to reveal a tropical island chain. "The Bahamas. Specifically..." She tapped the screen again and zoomed in on one of the islands. "Eleuthera." Darla squealed again. "I knew it."

"What?" Carter said, taking back the map.

"That we didn't go through all that just to steal a book."

Carter flashed a sly smile that shone through with mischief. "We're pirates now, Darla. It's always about the treasure."

A sudden dour cloud drifted over Carter and Darla and swallowed up the excitement, leaving them standing in puddles up to their ankles.

Brad. If ever there was a human rain cloud.

Make that a storm cloud. With lightning!

"Hate to ruin your grand adventure before it starts, but aren't you two forgetting something? That part where you're being shipped off to live with a family on the other side of the country, and I'm getting press-ganged to a military academy?"

For just a split second, Carter heard the crack in Brad's voice and saw it in his face. And in that crack he saw and heard everything he was trying not to feel.

Carter placed the map gently on his cot and grabbed his brother by the shoulders. He looked up into his eyes and lowered his voice. "None but the wrath of the kraken could tear this crew asunder." When Brad's expression went unchanged, Carter changed his voice. "We won't be separated, bro. You just gotta trust me. You do trust me, right?"

"No."

"Okay, I may have earned that. But you will." Carter's smile reached critical mischief. "Because I have a plan."

Brad gulped. For the first time since he learned he was being shipped off to a military academy, he now had something else to fear. Something much worse—one of his little brother's plans.

4

Darla emerged from her mother's bedroom just a minute after entering, her face pulled down in a frown. In the brief second before she spoke, Carter imagined his plan slamming into a rocky outcrop before even leaving the harbor.

Then she held up a set of keys and her face flipped into a smile. "Got 'em. She's out cold. Halfway through a new box of wine."

"Phase one complete," Carter said.

The three of them ran down the hall, down the stairs, and out the back door to the driveway. Darla tossed Brad the keys.

"Shotgun," Carter called.

"Yeah, right," Darla said as she shoved him out of the way and got in the front seat.

Brad slid into the driver's seat and looked at Carter in the mirror. "You realize the very first thing you asked me to do after telling me to trust you is steal a car?"

"I do," Carter answered. "But technically speaking, it's a van. Now, get this box moving."

Brad shook his head, started the van and shifted

into gear. Brad had only gotten his license a few weeks earlier, and it showed. He drove like an old lady. A paranoid old lady. The van moved at a snail's crawl but eventually reached its destination—a dark alley in a sketchy part of town.

"Seriously?" Brad's forehead fell against the steering wheel.

"Your yellow streak is starting to show through your shirt," Darla said.

Brad's frown sunk even lower.

"Relax, it'll be fine."

"Sure, it will. Because everything has been so fine thus far."

Carter poked his head into the front seat. "This is an essential part of the plan. How lucky are we that Darla has underworld connections?"

Brad shook his head and sighed as Darla stepped out of the van.

She stared into the dark, cocking her ear as though to listen. When she heard a rattle and a hissing sound, she smiled. "Iggy, Spritz, you there? It's me, Whitebread."

"Whitebread?" Carter and Brad asked in unison.

"It's my tagger name," she answered.

"Naturally," Brad said.

She flashed a mischievous smile over her shoulder. "Haven't done it in a while. There's a lot you don't know about me."

Carter punched Brad in the arm. "She's got history. You know what they say about a girl with history?"

Darla turned around and gave Carter a death-ray stare. "Tell me, Carter. What *do* they say about a girl with history?"

Carter's lip quivered. "Um... You know... History's cool."

"That's what I thought."

Suddenly, two figures emerged from the dark of the alley. They were teens, about the same age as Darla, fifteen or sixteen. Both wore dark hoodies and torn jeans. Both were covered with splotches of bright paint, making them look like two-legged, upright-walking psychedelic Dalmatians. They bumped knuckles with Darla, and then Spritz, a Latina with long black hair streaked with blue highlights, said, "Nice mom van. Bringing the kids to soccer practice?"

Iggy, an Asian boy with gauged ears, pointed at Brad behind the wheel. "That guy selling you insurance?"

Carter laughed hard in Brad's ear, which turned bright red.

"My boyfriend," Darla said.

Both taggers chuckled. Spritz made a comment Carter couldn't hear, but Darla immediately punched her in the shoulder.

"There's the Whitebread I know," Spritz said. "What you need, girl?"

"Your talents," Darla said.

"The canvas?" Iggy asked.

Darla pointed at the van.

"The ride or the boyfriend?" Spritz asked. "I'm good, not a miracle worker."

Darla punched her again. A moment later, she opened the passenger door and said, "They'll do it."

"Phase two complete," Carter said. "Now starts the hard stuff."

Brad sighed.

Ms. Roberts burst into the room just as the sun began to peek into the boys' bedroom. The door slammed open like a prison cell opening for the last time. "Wakey-wakey. Rise and shine." She had a sing-song quality to her voice, a Christmas morning glee. "Today's the day. The first day of the rest of my life."

"Don't you mean the rest of *our* lives?" Carter asked

"Get washed up," she sang as she danced out of the room. "No one likes a smelly orphan." And she was gone.

Carter and Brad kicked off their blankets. They were both fully dressed underneath, and hadn't slept a wink. They leapt out of bed. Brad pulled a large duffel bag out from under his bed while Carter rounded up everything they would need.

As Carter shoved some clothes into the bag, the door swung open and three of the residents of St. John's County Orphanage entered the room.

They were an eclectic bunch. But Carter wouldn't have grown up with any other kids had he been given the chance. They made life tolerable. Sometimes even fun.

Yvette, a fifteen-year-old Cuban, was not someone to be messed with. She'd given Brad more than his fair share of black eyes in the past five years, a few of which he deserved. Simply put, the girl took no crap. "I can't believe that evil hag is splitting you up." She slammed her fist into the palm of her hand. *Ella es una bruja!*

"It is what it is," Brad said as he resumed packing.

Marcus was the youngest of the three at fourteen, but he was the tallest. He was a black kid from Pittsburgh. He'd come down to Florida with his grandparents when he was five, but they'd both died a year later. He bounced around to a few homes, but never stayed long. His old-school fro poked out from under his Pittsburgh Pirates hat. "It sucks, but it is what it is."

Louis hadn't been in the house very long. He was only fourteen, but his parents kicked him out of the house when he came out to them last year. Carter often imagined dropping them in shark-infested waters.

His hair was shaved on one side and the rest hung past his ear on the other side. He clung to a pink Hello Kitty suitcase. He dabbed at the tears streaming down his cheeks with a pink Hello Kitty handkerchief. "I hate goodbyes. They're so...so..."

"Sucky."

"Thank you, Marcus. Wonderfully stated."

Carter stood defiantly in front of them and pulled his skull and crossbones hood over his head.

They rolled their eyes.

"Don't be countin' us out just yet," Carter said in his pirate voice. "Ain't a tide in all the seven seas strong enough to pull us apart."

He nearly choked on the last word, his pirate swagger faltering, when Linn appeared like a technicolor ghost in the doorway. She drifted into the room on a swell of watercolor—if that artist had dropped his glass of water on the easel and all the colors swirled together. She wore a bright orange Kentucky Derby hat, a green and purple summer dress with ruffles, and mismatched red and blue knee socks.

She stopped only inches from Carter. He suddenly became way too aware of his own body. His face felt warm. *Hot!* He didn't know what to do with his hands. Or his feet. Or his tongue. He'd forgotten how to speak. He wanted to pull his hood over his eyes.

"I heard you were leaving," Linn said.

"Uh-huh," was all Carter could force his mutinous tongue to say.

24

"I'm gonna miss you."

"Uh-huh."

"I hope we see each other again."

"Uh-huh."

And then the moment he'd dreamed of. She leaned in. *That* lean in. The one in movies where the soft music starts to play and everything moves in slow motion. Only Carter didn't hear any music. He heard the sound of his heart pounding in his ears. And things didn't slow down. They sped up and went sideways and tripped over themselves.

Her lips were just centimeters from touching his. Finally, he regained control of his body. He shot his hand forward and gripped hers in a firm handshake. "Take care of yourself."

Linn's frown would have made even the happiest clown sad. Her hand slipped out of Carter's sweaty palm. She wiped it on the ruffles of her dress as she walked out.

"Smooth," Brad said.

"Like a cheese grater," Marcus added. "Painful. Watching that hurt *me*."

"Whatever," Carter said. "The only girl for me is the sea," he added in his pirate voice, though it sounded half-hearted. He turned from the others to hide his reddening cheeks and noticed Darla walking across the yard, toward the next-door neighbor's house carrying a plate of cookies. The sight made him feel a little better.

"Phase three in progress," he said.

Brad rushed to the window to see. His cheeks reddened at the sight of her.

"You really think this will work?" Brad said, his voice full of longing.

"Absolutely," Carter answered. "Walter's geared up for big game. His equipment will hold."

Walter's yard looked like a junkyard of old fishing equipment. The fence was made of vintage fishing rods. The mailbox was a taxidermied tarpon. A dilapidated old fishing boat took up most of the driveway, though it never came out from under its tarp. Sitting in the middle of the yard was a huge chunk of raw meat—a rump roast from the looks of it—stuck through with a giant shark hook, which was tied to a length of braided fishing line that led through Walter's open window. Today's bait. It was ham yesterday—a whole freakin' ham!—but he didn't catch anything, so he must have changed it up. He didn't catch anything the day before either. Or the day before that. But there was always bait on that hook.

Stories about Walter had always swirled around the orphanage. The most common being that he once owned his own commercial fishing boat with a small crew. They were out one day, doing what they always do, when a massive shark took an interest in them. The shark circled the boat all day, scaring away the fish. When it came time to pack it in and head to shore, the shark had other ideas. Suddenly, every line on the boat jerked. A quick flash of excitement from the crew faded almost instantly when they realized that it wasn't a big pay day pulling—it was doom with a dorsal fin!

The boat was ripped in half. Walter was the only one to make it home, drifting back to shore on a scrap of hull. And he's been tossing hunks of meat out in his yard ever since, trying to catch that shark.

That's the story, anyway. Ms. Roberts always said he was just plain crazy.

The arrival of a Chevy Suburban with a camouflage paint job in the orphanage driveway drew Carter's eye from Walter's house. A pit formed in his stomach. "Crap. They're early."

Brad let out a sigh and hung his head. "Hey, you tried. Let's just get this over with."

"No way," Carter said. "That isn't happening. We'll go to Plan B. I always have a Plan B."

Brad brightened, hopeful. "Serve it up."

"As soon as it comes to me I'll let you know."

Brad's face sank.

Suddenly they heard the front door crash open and boots march on the tile floor of the foyer.

A booming voice shook the floor: "Bradley Humbolt front and center!"

Carter grabbed Brad's arm as his big brother walked for the door. He squeezed tighter than he's ever squeezed anything. "This can still work. You still trust me, right?"

Brad smiled at him, tousled his hair. "Never trust a pirate. You taught me that." And then he walked out.

Carter made to follow, but a horn honk outside drew him back to the window. "Now what?" he grumbled.

Pulling into the driveway behind the camo SUV was a powder blue vintage Rolls Royce, a car that looked straight out of one of those classic movies where women are always swooning and there are a lot of tight close-ups.

Like the car, the woman who stepped out of the door held open by her chauffeur looked like she stepped out of the past. She was in her seventies, wore a bright yellow Kentucky Derby hat that shone like the sun, her face was hidden behind octagonal sunglasses, and she carried a golden parasol. She looked like an Andy Warhol painting of an aristocratic British lady.

"An ill wind," Carter mumbled, and then ran downstairs.

Brad had already fallen in line by the time Carter reached the foyer.

Major North of the Valley Forge Military Academy towered over everyone. Brad nearly disappeared in the shadow of the man's pectorals. He looked like an extra from *Predator*—bulky, chiseled from granite, like he could survive in the jungle while being hunted by aliens. At least until the second act.

Two of his academy cadets stood at attention behind him. They were identical twins, which took a second and third glance to confirm considering there were both in uniform and had shaved heads.

"Every morning will begin with two hours of PT," Major North barked. "Followed by two hours of marching in place." He leaned over, put his face only inches from Brad's. "You will follow orders without question. Or you will know pain."

Ms. Roberts stood next to Brad, smiling like a hyena at Major North. "You're strict."

"Discipline is the backbone of every young man," Major North said. "Without discipline, he is nothing more than a useless sack of goo." He turned back to Brad and barked, "Do you want to be a goo-sack, son?"

"No, sir!" Brad barked back, his voice cracking.

Ms. Roberts ran her finger down the major's arm. "I know a little something about discipline. There are some that still know me as Mistress Jane."

The front door swung open again, and another elephant joined the circus. A man in a suit who looked like he hadn't farted in forty years stood just inside the door. His mustache hid his entire mouth, so it seemed like his voice came from nowhere. "Presenting, Mrs. Phyllis Katzenbacher."

The woman who emerged from the Rolls Royce walked in like she expected everyone to bow.

Ms. Roberts nearly did. "Mrs. Katzenbacher, welcome. Thank you so much for coming."

"This establishment is quite dreadful," Mrs. Katzenbacher said. "I feel like I'm getting hepatitis just standing here."

"I can assure you, all the children have had their shots," Ms. Roberts said. "Major North," she said, turning to the hulking man, "This is Phyllis Katzenbacher, one of the wealthiest women in the country."

Phyllis cast a sideways glance at Ms. Roberts like she were a swamp creature emerging from the muck. "Yes, I'm quite rich. Now, if you please, fetch the child for whom I came."

Carter sunk back around the corner to the kitchen.

"It's high time we be on our way, as well," Major North said. "Cadets, fetch Humbolt's belongings."

Everything was going wrong. No, not wrong, just in a different order. A pirate was beholden to no plan that couldn't be rewritten. This could still work.

But he had to act fast. Avoiding Ms. Roberts's searching eyes and the marching cadets, Carter took the backstairs up to his room.

He remembered the memory of his mother. The words Mr. Croce wrote in his book.

By all the salt in the sea, he would not lose his family this day.

Everything went dark. Not a shred of light. Carter used that to his advantage. Pretended to be asleep. Footsteps outside. Calm, relaxed, don't move.

He took a deep breath and let it out as slowly as he could.

Suddenly, he was weightless, drifting through the air.

Muffled voices sounded from all around, like they came straight out of the darkness.

"Man, this thing is heavy," said one of the twin cadets. "You got a dead body in here, Humbolt?"

Brad tried to force a laugh.

Carter unzipped the bag from the inside, just enough to peek out. They were in the foyer now.

"Roll out," Major North commanded. Brad made to turn but was suddenly slammed into by a petite frame covered in a skull and crossbones hoodie.

She's good, Carter thought as he watched Linn sob into his brother's chest. He'd had only seconds to explain to her what was happening before the cadets stormed into his room. He wasn't even sure she'd agreed before he stuffed himself inside Brad's duffel bag.

Linn ran past Brad, out the door, sobbing. Carter hoped he'd see her again. His cheeks burned when he thought of their near-kiss.

Phyllis and her chauffeur followed Linn without a word.

Brad followed the major out, and the cadets brought up the rear.

Ms. Roberts whistled a joyful tune behind them.

Carter spied the Rolls Royce tear out of the driveway like the occupants had just stolen something. And then he saw another figure crash into Brad's chest.

"Is this goodbye?" Darla said, choking back sobs.

"No, never," Brad said. It's `I'll see you soon'."

"Don't count on it," Ms. Roberts said, her voice still singing.

Brad and Darla pressed together again, her lips nearly touching his ear, whispering something to him.

Brad climbed into the Suburban. The cadets threw the duffel into the trunk.

And then they were moving. So many moving parts. Barely controlled chaos. But that's where pirates thrived. The illusion of chaos was their greatest weapon. Make everyone think they were out of control, and use the fog of turmoil to take what they wanted.

Carter moved a little, careful not to make noise, trying to relieve the cramping in his legs. He pressed his nose to the open hole in the zipper, trying to breathe some air that hadn't been circulating near Brad's underwear.

Then he tensed in anticipation.

Any second now.

Any second.

Wait for—

The SUV jerked violently. Carter rolled forward and slammed into the back of the seat. A loud, metallic shriek pierced his ears.

The truck stopped.

Major North screamed a steady stream of obscenities. The doors opened. Everyone shouted. Carter's ears still rung and his head hurt.

Maybe he had a concussion. He couldn't see! Everything was black! Oh no! He was blind!

No, wait—he suddenly remembered ... *Duh! I'm in a duffel bag.*

A duffel bag that was suddenly hoisted into the air and moving fast.

Carter unzipped the bag enough to stick his head out. Brad was wearing the duffel like a backpack and running through the woods from the scene of the wreck. The rear axle of the SUV had been completely ripped off. Attached to it, a giant shark hook and a hunk of beef.

"This doesn't mean I trust you," Brad said through huffs and puffs.

"Says the guy not currently cleaning a toilet with his toothbrush."

They exited the small patch of forest onto a residential street in the neighborhood just up the road from the orphanage. And if everything went according to plan...

"There it is," Brad said, pointing to the unrecognizable orphanage van. Iggy and Spritz hid it perfectly under a coat of graffiti.

"Uh oh," Carter said.

"What uh oh?"

"Just keep running," Carter said as he unzipped the bag further.

Running up behind them were the two cadets, purpose in their eyes and discipline in their guts.

Carter pressed his feet into Brad's back. "The captain always goes down with the ship." He spring-boarded off Brad and slammed into the cadets, whose heads bounced off the pavement. "Go on without me," Carter said, lying on top of the dazed cadets. "I go to meet Davy Jones this day."

"Get up, idiot." Brad yanked Carter to his feet, and the two sprinted for the van.

Darla was waiting in the driver's seat. She leaned over to Brad as he climbed in.

"Save the kissy stuff for later," Carter said, pointing to the two recovering cadets through the windshield.

As the van pulled away, and the orphanage and Major North and the crazy rich lady fell behind, Carter felt like he could breathe again. The last hour happened so fast he barely had time to think.

He was so tired. He stretched his legs and lay down on the pile of blankets in the back of the van—and nearly peed his pants when the pile moved. He lifted the edge of the blanket, and three sets of eyes looked back at him. Carter kept quiet, assuming any more surprises would cause Brad to have an embolism, or go insane and squeeze Carter's head until his eyes popped.

The smell of salt and the sound of seabirds grew stronger with every passing second. Soon, they crossed the short bridge that led to the Camachee Island Marina. The cove had direct access to the intracoastal waterway, St. Augustine Inlet, and the Atlantic Ocean. In other words: freedom.

Oh, and boats. Lots and lots of boats.

The tires squealed as Darla pulled into the marina

parking lot and slammed on the brakes. She and Brad got out and opened the back so Carter could follow.

When he didn't move, Brad said, "Let's go. We can't waste time."

Carter sucked in a breath through his teeth. The lump of blankets at his feet felt like a land mine that, if disturbed, would blow everything to pieces. "Just so you know, it's not my fault."

Brad was perplexed. "What are you talking about?"

Carter pulled the blanket away, revealing Marcus, Yvette, and Louis.

"Hey," they said in unison.

Brad's jaw dropped. He marched away from the van, arms flailing in the air like they'd suddenly become separate from his body. "No. No way ever. Not a chance."

"What's a pirate without a crew?" Carter said, climbing over the pile of friends to exit the van.

"More like, what's a criminal without accomplices?" Brad said. "Because that's exactly what we are. Criminals. We stole a car. Destroyed another. And—"

"Technically, we stole *a van*. And technically, we destroyed *an SUV*," Carter corrected.

"Technically, you're an idiot," Brad said with a snarl. "And I'm an even bigger idiot for listening to you. And now, you want to…" His voice drifted away as he looked out over the water.

"Steal a boat," Darla finished the sentence for him.

Brad spun and pointed a stern finger at all of them. "We are *not* stealing a boat."

"Then what are we *not* doing here?" Carter asked. "Why come to the marina in the first place? You knew the plan. This was always the goal. Always."

Brad paced the pavement. He looked at the black beneath his feet, then at the blue sky above his head. He reached into his pocket and pulled out a keychain, a trinket that he always had with him. He rubbed it absently with his thumb. "I'm just trying to keep you safe, Carter. I told her I would. I promised."

A rogue wave of feeling slammed into Carter's chest. Grief, sadness, gratitude. It all mixed together. He stepped to his brother. "You can't keep me safe if we're on separate sides of the country. This is the only way we stay together."

"The only way *we all* stay together," Darla added.

Brad looked at each of them, the ragtag bunch of orphans and runaways he had grown up with. Rogues, all of them.

"Face it, bro," Yvette said. "This is your family."

"All for one and all that," from Marcus.

"That's musketeer speak, not pirate," Carter corrected.

"Musketeers, pirates, tomato, tomatoe," Marcus said with a shrug.

"We're family any way you slice it," Louis chimed in.

"*Una familia de bichos raros no deseados,*" Yvette said with a chuckle. "A family of unwanted oddballs."

"And families stick together," Carter said, extending his hand. "No matter how odd or unwanted."

Brad clasped his brother's hand in a half-hearted embrace. "They used to hang pirates once they caught them, you know."

Carter smiled. "Then we won't get caught."

"And...fade to black," Louis said as he wiped away a tear. "Beautiful, you guys. You made me feel some serious feels right there."

"Yeah, except nothing's fading yet. We still need a boat," Yvette reminded them. "And the gate is locked up tight."

Her thought was punctuated by a loud bang.

Marcus stood by the now-open gate, brandishing his bat. "Nah, it's open. Totally found it like this."

There was no time to laugh. The group ran through the open gate and onto the docks.

They all slammed on the brakes before slamming into Carter, who had stopped short. He marveled at a fifty-eight-foot Rossborough Ketch. With its polished teak gunwales and thick, tall masts, it looked straight out of the Golden Age of Piracy.

It spoke to him.

"This is it," Carter said. "This is our pirate ship."

6

Meanwhile...
Ashore, far from the adventure on the high seas, but never far from adventure...

Phyllis blinked her brightly painted eyes at the child sitting on the far end of the leather bench seat in the back of her Rolls Royce.

The child blinked back.

"You are *not* a boy," Phyllis said.

"I am not," Linn said. "Thank you for noticing."

Phyllis stared a while longer, perhaps trying to wrap her head around the odd turn of events. "Jeeves," she eventually called to her driver. "Bring us back to the orphanage posthaste. This is not the child I ordered."

The vintage luxury car swung around and headed back to where they'd come from.

Linn made a sweeping motion with her hand, gesturing from Phyllis's hat to her shoes. "I love your ensemble."

Phyllis scoffed. "I am absurdly wealthy, child, and am thus immune to flattery." As she spoke, she ran her hands down the length of her dress, flattening out the wrinkles, realizing, obviously, that her ensemble was quite outstanding.

Linn removed her Carter disguise and unzipped her backpack. "If you don't mind, ma'am, I'd love to get out of this drab outfit." She pulled her derby hat and blindingly bright dress from her bag.

Phyllis slid her octagonal sunglasses down the bridge of her nose. She admired the outfit, and then looked at Linn as if for the first time. "You know, I'm thinking of having my tearoom repainted. What hue would you choose?"

Phyllis's tone said it all. This wasn't just a question, it was a test.

"Vermillion," Linn said without a moment's hesitation. "Perhaps some eggplant polka dots as well. A tearoom should be bold."

Phyllis sat back, folded her hands across her lap, looking impressed. It wasn't often that she was at a loss for words, but she was now.

After a long moment of deep thought: "Is there anyone at that awful orphanage who would miss you terribly if you weren't to return?"

Linn looked down at the skull and crossbones hoodie. "No," she sighed.

"Then we best be on our way," Phyllis said. "Jeeves, you dunce, turn this car around. The airport is in the complete opposite direction." She opened a compartment in the seat between her and Linn and removed a sparkling water. "Life is short." She handed the bottle to Linn, and removed another for herself. "Best not to spend it around people who don't appreciate you or a good color palette." She held her water toward Linn, and they clinked bottles.

"Agreed," Linn said.

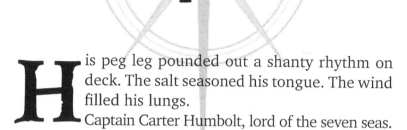

His peg leg pounded out a shanty rhythm on deck. The salt seasoned his tongue. The wind filled his lungs.

Captain Carter Humbolt, lord of the seven seas. The world was his.

"Weigh anchor," he yelled. "Hoist the mizzen. Get us to sea or feel my blade at yer throats. A storm's a-comin' and its name be Carter Humbolt! I'll chain the kraken to our bow, tame the tides themselves. The sea is mine!"

"Uh, Carter?" Yvette pointed at a console. "You just need to turn the power on."

Despite the ketch's retro look, it had all the modern-day amenities of any of today's ships, including a powerful engine.

"And you might want to save the 'sea is mine' talk until we at least get away from the dock," Darla said.

Carter cleared the pirate from his voice. "Right, totally." He pressed the power button, and the engine roared to life. "Arrr," he said quietly to himself, and his smile stretched all the way to the horizon.

The boat inched away from the dock, Yvette at the

helm. She was the only one who actually knew her way around a boat. Not that Carter minded. He couldn't stop staring out at…everything. The sun dancing on the water. The ripples on the ocean's surface, how they distorted the world above. The sails of all the passing sailboats as they fluttered in the breeze. The birds dipping and soaring. The horizon and everything just on the other side of it.

He didn't know how far they traveled before Yvette cut the engines. The harbor was long behind them. So was the orphanage and Ms. Roberts and the Valley Forge Military Academy. For the first time in a long time (maybe ever) he felt free.

"So now we're in the middle of the ocean," Brad said. "How long before we start eating each other?"

"Now that you mention it, I am rather hungry," Louis said, rubbing his stomach. "Did anyone bring sandwiches?"

"We can worry about food once we find Eleuthera," Darla said. "How far is it, anyway?"

"No idea," Yvette said. "I don't even know if we're going the right way. We need a compass or something. Some maps."

The conversation quickly devolved into a chaotic mass of voices, everyone talking over each other. And quicker than the wind changes, they were arguing. Just like everyone always argued. The way people argued on land where they had curfews and grownups told them what to do and drill sergeants tried to send them to war and parents were dead and they had nothing to call their own.

But they were at sea now.

"Avast ye!" Carter shouted.

The arguing stopped immediately. Only the sound of the water lapping against the hull.

He held a pen and Louis's pink Hello Kitty journal high. "The old rules hold no sway here. We make our own rules now. Our own code. *The pirate code.* No one telling us what to do."

"Sounds like someone's telling us what to do," Marcus grumbled.

"Ms. Roberts told us what to do," Carter said. "The police told us what to do. Foster parents told us what to do before getting rid of us." He swung the pen like a sword at the mention of each. "They never asked us what *we* wanted. They never cared. This code is us deciding for ourselves how we want to live."

"Democracy in its purest form," Darla said.

"Aye, lass," Carter answered. "By the people and for the people. Of course." He pointed to himself. "There does have to be a captain."

"Just read the code," Brad said.

Carter climbed atop a seat and used Yvette's shoulder to steady himself. He opened the notebook and cleared his throat. "Everyone shall obey their commander in all respects."

"Yup, like I said," Marcus grumbled.

Carter continued. "No one shall give, or dispose of, the ship's provisions, but everyone shall have an equal share. Everyone shall have an equal vote in all matters, at sea or on land. Everyone shall keep watch night and day and always be ready to man their stations. No one shall go ashore 'till the ship is in readiness to put to sea. All plunder shall be divided equally."

He hopped off the seat, and set the book on a nearby table. He signed first, then left the pen resting in the binding. "Make your marks."

One by one, the others signed. Brad scoffed the whole time, but whatever.

Marcus held the pen tip to paper, but looked up at Carter before signing. "Obey?"

Carter shrugged. "Yeah, or, you know, *take into consideration*?"

"And who decides the captain?" Marcus asked.

"We vote," Carter said.

Marcus nodded, seemingly pacified, and signed his name.

Carter snatched up the notebook. "Any who offends these articles shall be disciplined swiftly, the punishment to be decided by the crew." He snapped it shut. "We are now officially buccaneers."

8

Meanwhile...
'Neath a crewcut and aviator sunglasses, the by-the-book military man Major North sought his prey. His biceps thirsted for justice. His delts hungered for retribution. For he was a man who took his duty seriously. And someone had stepped in his duty.

Heh. Duty.

The cadets tore through the Humbolt boys' room at the orphanage with all the vigor of a pack of coyotes in a chicken coop. They left no stone unturned, no pillow with its insides intact, no mattress unflipped. Simply put, they gutted the place.

They were only distracted long enough to glance through the adult magazine found under the older boy's bed. Ms. Roberts, who insisted on escorting the major wherever he went, blushed at the sight of it. Major North snatched it from the boys.

That sort of thing is against regulation.

"This happen often?" Ms. Roberts asked. "Boys running away, I mean. I imagine it does. Happens here all the time. I was thinking about getting a dog. Maybe a pack. You know, to sic on them. Like in *Cool Hand Luke* or those other prison break movies."

Major North cocked an eyebrow and, if possible, stood even more rigid than he had before. "Never. I've never lost a cadet, ma'am. No man left behind. The Humbolt boy is under my command, and I will find him." He relaxed his stance a bit, tried to seem sympathetic. It was something he was working on, being more relatable to civilians. "And I will retrieve your daughter as well, ma'am."

"Huh?" Ms. Roberts looked up from Major North's arms in a daze. "Oh, right. Her. Yes, please. She needs to tell me where my van is." She sidled up beside Major North, ran her finger down his muscular arm. "Maybe once we find it, I can give you a tour of the area. It has a very spacious backseat."

A shiver ran up the major's spine, and his gut bubbled. Civilians. More trouble than they're worth.

"Found something!" one of the cadets exclaimed.

Major North sighed with relief at having an excuse to move away from Ms. Roberts and her wandering hands. "Show me what you've got, cadet."

The cadet removed a piece of paper from a dog-eared and well-read copy of *Treasure Island* from the younger Humbolt's bookshelf. Covered in scribbles and notes, it looked to be a hand drawn map.

The cadet squinted at it. "Looks like an island. Someplace called Urethra."

Major North winced. "Eleuthera," he corrected. "Once this mission is over, you two are getting less PT, and more book time."

He snatched the paper from the cadet's hand. He studied the notes in the margins, the diagrams, plans and backup plans. This kid was smart, strategic. He'd make a fine addition to the Valley Forge Military Academy one day.

"Eleuthera is an island in the Bahamas chain," Major North said. "I did a training dive there once when I was in the service." He folded the paper and stuck it in his pocket. "They ran toward the marina. I'm guessing they had a boat waiting for them." He clenched his fist. His biceps bulged under his shirt. "That's definitely where they're heading. So that's where we're heading. Cadets," he barked in a commanding voice.

They snapped to attention.

"Roll out. We're off to the Bahamas."

"Valley Forge Military Academy. Hoo-rah!"

eing a pirate in practice is much different than being a pirate in theory. They had their ship. They signed the articles. They were at sea. Done, right? Let the pirating begin.

Wrong!

So laughably, foolishly wrong. You should be ashamed of yourself.

Pirates needed plunder. They needed food. Worst of all, or maybe most importantly, they needed direction. Because when you set six rogues adrift on a boat without direction, that's all they do—drift.

Yvette familiarized herself with the controls of the boat while the others just...kind of hung around.

Louis clutched his rumbling stomach. Marcus smacked his bat in his hand. Brad hadn't stopped grumbling and whining for as long as Carter could remember. And they were all staring at him.

"What?" Carter finally blurted out.

"I thought being a pirate would be a little more exciting," Louis said. "And, I don't know, maybe there'd be sandwiches. Or at least some finger foods."

"I thought it'd be less boring," Marcus said. "This is boring. *Really* boring. Why is this so boring?"

"Because you're boring," Carter said. "Only boring people get bored."

"Why are we just sitting here?" Marcus grumbled.

"Yvette's getting comfortable with the boat," Carter answered.

"And what do we do after?" Marcus said. "Where do we go?"

"To Eleuthera," Carter said. "You know, that way somewhere." He pointed to the horizon.

Brad stood up, looking like all he wanted to do was push Carter overboard. "This isn't a game anymore," Brad said. "So stop treating it like one."

"I'm not," Carter said. His cheeks got hot.

"You're still playing pirate," Brad argued. "All you ever do is play. You don't take anything seriously. Well, that's not an option anymore. Because you've dragged us all into this."

Carter willed himself not to cry. He forced the hurt to turn into anger. "Why don't you just jump overboard and swim back to shore? You don't have what it takes to serve on my crew."

"*Your* crew?" Brad scoffed. He jabbed his hand into his pocket and took out an old keychain he always carried with him. He rubbed it with his thumb, like it was a magic lamp, and he was hoping for a genie.

"Yeah," Carter shot back. "*My* crew. I broke into the museum. I stole the map. I got you out of the military academy. And all you've done the entire time is whine. Whine, whine, whine."

"And all I've done your entire life is keep you alive. Alive! Alive! Alive! But I'm strongly reconsidering that."

47

Louis interjected, "I thought we were supposed to vote on a captain."

"No," Brad said. "I'm the oldest and probably the only one who isn't crazy. I'm in charge."

"Like hell you are!" Carter yelled. "You'll just bring us home. So afraid to break a rule."

Brad stepped forward, fist cocked back. He would have leveled his brother had Darla not intervened.

She put a hand on Brad's chest. "Take it easy. This last day has been crazy. I think we could all use a little rest, something to eat. Let's do that. And then we'll decide our next steps."

Brad nodded.

"Sound good?" she said to Carter with a smile meant to soothe him.

It worked, in part. But the other part of him was still pissed. He nodded anyway and marched off toward the bow.

It was quiet. Painfully quiet. It reminded Carter of curfew at the orphanage. No sound after lights out.

"I'll see if there's anything in the kitchen," Louis said. "Galley, I mean. That's what they're called, right, Carter?"

Carter didn't answer.

Louis walked below deck. The others followed.

Carter sat alone, looking out at the sea.

Darla emerged from below deck twenty minutes later.

Carter hadn't moved. He was afraid to. Afraid that if he went below, he'd walk in on Brad convincing them all that they needed to head back to shore, that the game was over.

"Louis found some food," Darla said. "The kitchen is actually pretty stocked."

"Galley," Carter said, his voice barely a whisper.

"Right," Darla laughed.

The silence echoed off the water again.

Darla rubbed Carter's back. A gesture to say, *It's okay.*

There were times, a lot of them, when Carter wished Darla was his sister and Brad was just another orphan. She knew how to make him feel better. Brad knew how to yell at him or call him reckless or treat him like a baby.

"He's just worried," Darla said.

"He's always worried," Carter said.

"Can you blame him?"

Her response surprised Carter. Of course he could blame him. He was blaming him right now. They finally had their chance to get free of Ms. Roberts and the orphanage and the whole system and their wretched lives. Only Brad didn't want to. He wanted to follow the rules. He wanted to go back. Go back to how things were.

How could he not blame him?

"With you for a brother, I'd always be worried," Darla said.

The hurt and anger swirled inside Carter again. He wanted to kick her overboard now, too. She and Brad could go find a deserted island somewhere and kiss all day long and build a shanty made of palm leaves and die of exposure or get eaten by wild boars or—

"Because what would life be like without you in it?"

Wait, what?

Carter blinked back the tears as he looked at Darla. Her face was silhouetted by the sun setting behind her.

"He's been terrified of losing you since the day you

guys lost your mother." She took Carter's hand. "And you don't make it easy on him. I mean, look where we are. On a stolen boat, in the middle of ocean, following a stolen map to find pirate treasure in the Bahamas. If one single part of this crazy plan goes south, then you go both right back into the system. But, he'll probably go into a different system."

Carter knew what she meant. Brad's old enough. He'd probably get jail time. Carter's cheeks burned hot. Shame flooded his lungs, making it hard to take a deep breath.

"So, try to take it easy on him, okay?" Darla squeezed Carter's hand, and then let go. "He's doing the best he can." She walked away, stopping at the top of the stairs that led below deck. "And come down for dinner."

Carter took a last look out at the water. It was getting dark. He wouldn't be able to see it soon. Once the sun went down, all he'd have was the boat and the people on it.

He followed Darla below deck.

He stopped at the bottom of the stairs to take the place in. He knew at that moment that he absolutely chose the right boat to steal. This place was amazing. There was a bed that took up the entire bow where Yvette and Marcus sat cross-legged, shoveling food into their mouths. A proper dining room table sat against the wall, anchored to it and the floor. Padded benches lined the long sides of the table. Brad sat on one, eating soup from a bowl, not looking up. An unclaimed bowl of soup sat across from him.

Louis had found an apron that said "Kiss the Captain" and donned it proudly as he stirred a pot atop the stove. The boat was outfitted with a kitchenette— stove, microwave, even a dishwasher.

This thing was nicer than the orphanage.

"Soup's on," Louis said. "Although I guess I'd call it more of a chowder, if we're being technical. The pantry in here is fantastic. I never had anything like this to work with back home. I tried one time, and Ms. Roberts totally flipped. Could be that I almost burned the place down..."

"We get it," Yvette said. "You cook."

Louis shot her a sharp stare, which she ignored by lying down.

"Smells good," Carter said, sitting across from Brad.

Brad didn't look up. But as Carter lifted a big spoonful toward his mouth, he said, "It's got onions in it. Big ones. You can pick them out if you have to."

Carter looked down at his spoon and was horrified by the huge chunk of vile root vegetable looking up at him. "Thanks," he said, flicking it off his spoon.

Brad smiled but never looked up from his bowl.

The rest of the night didn't feel real. They laughed, even found some cards and played a round of poker. Only two of them actually knew how to play. But there was a radio. They cranked it as loud as they wanted and belted out song after song. They danced. They threw things and didn't pick up after themselves. They didn't do the dishes even though there was a dishwasher.

They did whatever they wanted and nothing they didn't. And they did it together.

But, after a while, their eyelids grew heavy.

"I need to crash," Yvette said through a yawn.

The rest agreed.

"Dibs on the bed," Yvette called, and then flopped onto the mattress.

"Girls get the bed," Darla yelled and dove next to her.

The boys laid out some blankets on the floor. One of the benches along the wall actually pulled out into a single bed. Brad took that. Of course.

"Wait," Carter said. "Shouldn't someone keep watch?"

"For what?" Marcus said.

"Other boats," Carter answered. "I mean, we are technically fugitives, right? What if the Coast Guard finds us?"

"Good idea," Brad said. "I nominate you. Good night."

The rest agreed.

Carter grumbled, rubbed the sleep from his eyes, and marched up top. He sat in the captain's chair, tried to familiarize himself with the controls. He looked out at the water, but saw nothing but black and the reflection of the moon.

The rhythmic sound of water lapping against the hull was like a lullaby.

Carter's head snapped up suddenly. He'd fallen asleep. What time was it? How long had he been out?

What had woken him up?

The sound of an idling engine. Just off the stern.

10

He couldn't see it, but Carter knew it was there. The sound of its engine carried on the water, but it was barely a hum. Just resting, watching. It couldn't have been far.

Their lights weren't on. Not even a beacon to let passing boats know where it is.

Carter's gut pinched.

He slid out of the captain's chair and snuck below deck as quietly as he could. He stepped over Marcus and Louis, to the pull-out bed. "Brad," he whispered, shaking his brother awake.

"What is it?" Brad's voice was full of sleep, and he hadn't even opened his eyes.

"Someone's outside," Carter said. "A boat."

Brad shot upright. "Coast Guard?"

"I don't think so," Carter said. "They haven't identified themselves. Haven't even turned their lights on. But I hear them."

The others began to stir.

"What's going on?" Louis asked. "Was it the chowder? Did I poison you? I knew I shouldn't have used that can of smoked oysters. It expired last month."

"Eww, but no," Carter said. "Someone's here."

Darla and Brad pressed their faces to the portholes, looking for any sign of another boat. They saw nothing, but they heard the idling engine just as Carter had.

"Something's not right," Brad said.

"Definitely not," Marcus agreed. "We should book. Slam on the gas, girl," he said to Yvette.

"Doesn't work like that," she said. "I need to fire up the engines first. Can't just peel out of here."

"Well, we can't just sit here," Brad said.

The crew paced for what felt like a lifetime. Carter immediately pondered every worst-case scenario. Maybe Ms. Roberts chartered a boat. She was a spiteful sort of person. But she wasn't adventurous. Maybe she hired a bounty hunter. No, she didn't have that kind of money. What if it didn't have anything to do with Ms. Roberts at all?

That scared Carter more. The thought of something totally unknown, just sitting out there in the dark.

He quickly pushed those thoughts aside. Now wasn't the time for fear. Now was the time when a pirate's true mettle was tested. To sail into the unknown. To tread in uncharted lands. To peer over the edge of the world. To stare into the abyss and laugh. This was the moment when *real* pirates were made.

But, despite some preconceptions, the real pirate legends weren't brutes. They were tacticians. Some quite brilliant. Brilliant enough that they never needed to raise their sword to plunder a prize ship, or protect their own ship. He hoped this was one such occasion.

He paced the length of the boat, taking stock of everything that may be of use—pots and pans, a stocked kitchen, scuba equipment, nautical gear. He looked at them like puzzle pieces, rearranged them in his mind and put them back together in the most pirate-y of fashions.

A smile lit on Carter's face. A smile that immediately put a skeptical frown on Brad's.

"Do you trust me?" Carter said.

Brad sighed. "Here we go again."

Carter, Brad, and Darla climbed the stairs to the deck after Carter laid out his plan. There was still a twinge in Carter's gut, but now it was much less fear and much more anticipation.

Brad walked out on the bow and maneuvered the spotlight affixed there. Darla flipped it on.

Two men winced and shielded their eyes from the light. They stood aboard a thirty-foot speedboat, a sleek and luxurious looking piece of modern equipment. The men looked as obnoxious as the vessel they commanded. Hawaiian shirts. Gold chains on their necks and wrists. Sunglasses on top of their heads. Even in the pale light of the moon, their tans were deep and orange. Open collars and buttons showed thick tufts of gross old man chest hair.

"Whoa, you caught us," one of the men said. "Consider me embarrassed, right, Nestor?"

The other man, Nestor, flashed a smiled. "Absolutely, JJ. Caught red-handed."

"Caught doing what?" Darla asked, voice tight with caution.

"Checking out your boat, of course," JJ said. "It's a real beauty. We caught sight of it earlier. When we came up on it a few minutes ago, we couldn't help but take the opportunity to have a closer look."

"But we figured you'd all be sleeping," Nestor quickly added. "Didn't want to flash our lights and wake you."

Brad nodded. From the corner of Carter's eye, he could see that his big brother was actually considering this fish turd stew of a story. Brad... Brad... Brad... "When did you say you caught sight of us?" Carter asked, obviously unconvinced. "We haven't seen any boats since we hit open water."

"On your way out of port," Nestor said.

"Which one?" Carter pressed.

JJ and Nestor looked at each other. An unspoken conversation passed between them. "Your parents up?" Nestor asked.

"No," Brad said. "Still sleeping."

"Why don't you wake them?" JJ said, the congeniality fading from his voice. "We'd love to chat with them about the boat. Maybe come aboard and get a look under the hood." He smiled, but Carter saw the knife's edge in it.

"State yer business matter-of-fact," Carter growled at the men. "What is it ye want? And just know that ye'll never be steppin' foot on this here ship."

The two men laughed.

"Get a load of this kid," JJ said, nudging Nestor. "Thinks he's Jack Sparrow."

Carter gestured to JJ's outfit. "Do you think you're Crockett or Tubbs?"

"Isn't *Miami Vice* a little before your time?" JJ responded.

"Netflix, bro," Carter said.

Darla stepped to the edge of the boat, getting between the two sets of men. "Listen, it's late. Why don't we all just go on our way? If we cross paths again when our parents are awake, then you can talk to them. I'm sure they'd love to have you aboard."

"Listen, sweetheart," Nestor said, "why don't you just hush up and let us talk to the man of the boat, there." He pointed at Brad.

"Oh, screw this guy," Darla said through clenched teeth.

"Man of the boat, my butt," Carter said through the same.

Now Brad stepped forward, pulled Darla back from leaping across the open water and punching the strange men in the neck. "I think it's best if you move on."

"And don't let the fair winds whip yer overly tanned hides on the way out," Carter added.

Nestor scratched at his chin. He looked Carter up and down, studied him like he was a specimen. "What's with you, kid?"

"I'm a pirate," Carter answered matter-of-factly. "And, as such, I'll tolerate no lip from jelly-boned squibs like you."

All pretense fell from Nestor's face. His mouth turned down into a scowl. His eyes darkened. "A pirate."

"Kid's a bit behind the times," JJ said, a laugh in his voice, but not one born from humor. "Pirates don't talk like that anymore."

"What would ye know about it?" Carter asked.

Nestor and JJ raised their hands, which, until then, had been hidden behind their backs. Each held a semiautomatic handgun.

"Quite a bit," Nestor said. "We're pirates, too."

Carter's stomach leapt into his throat. Every instinct told him to hit the deck, to run, to scream, to cry. He did none of those things. Because he pushed those instincts aside until one came by that served him.

He put one foot on the edge of the boat, dug his fists into his hips, and pressed his chest out. "This here vessel's our home. And no picaroons will chase us from it."

Brad slapped his hand over Carter's mouth. "Don't mind him. He's got issues."

"Don't we all," Nestor said as he pulled the action back on his gun. "Now, unless you also want plenty of holes that God didn't give you, step aside."

Carter dug his fists in deeper, stuck his chest out further. It was uncomfortable. "I prefer a merry life and a short one over one spent cowering to dogs like you."

"If that's what you prefer," Nestor said.

The silence of the open sea exploded in a burst of fire and thunder. Light danced across Carter's vision. Screaming echoed from all around. Carter couldn't tell where it came from—his own mouth or those around him.

Until he realized that he couldn't have screamed. He clenched his mouth shut. He kept his chest out and his eyes open. He refused to give those soulless wannabe pirates the satisfaction.

A barrage of bullets hit the water just off the ketch's hull, spraying seawater into the air. When the shooting stopped, Carter realized that his heart also stopped beating. He stopped breathing. He didn't blink. It had only been a second. It felt like a lifetime.

Seawater rained down on him.

Brad and Darla had hit the deck. But Carter hadn't moved.

"Ye've yet to impress," he said through a cutting grin. Then he raised one hand high. "Allow me to show you how it's done."

JJ and Nestor laughed deep and heartily. So heartily that they didn't notice the portholes snap open.

"On my signal, unleash hell," Carter ordered.

The men laughed harder. So hard they didn't notice the scuba tanks loaded like cannonballs into each of the open portholes.

Carter dropped his hand. "Fire!"

From below deck, he heard his orders being carried out. Louis, Yvette, and Marcus smashed the nozzles off each of the tanks. The gas shot into the boat, propelling the tanks outward like silver missiles.

The fools' laughter was cut short. One of the tanks slammed Nestor square in the chest. Another hit JJ's shoulder, spinning him like a top before he hit the deck. The third tank punched a hole straight through the fiberglass hull of their fancy-pants speedboat.

Water flooded through the gaping hole, and the speedboat began to tip.

Nestor gasped for air, struggled to stand. JJ yelled in pain each time he tried to move his arm. Dislocated shoulder, most likely.

Hard to swim if you can't breathe and your arm's busted.

Carter stood triumphant, gripping a line with one hand so he could lean over the edge and talk down to his humiliated foes. "You aren't pirates. It's men like you who put men such as me to sailing under the black flag." He stared down at them as the water rushed up around their ankles, knees, hips. Then he turned to his crew, all of whom had joined him topside. "Save the drowning bilge rats," he ordered.

The crew looked stunned.

"Seriously?" Marcus asked. "These guys just tried to kill us. I thought we took no quarter and gave no quarter."

"That's not the kind of pirate I want to be," Carter said. "Not the kind of pirate like them, anyway." He gestured to the floundering miscreants below.

Two life jackets splashed into the water. Darla looked proud to have tossed them. "Not the kind of pirate I want to be, either."

Murmurs of agreement passed among the crew.

"But don't mistake our mercy for weakness," Carter called to Nestor and JJ as they scrambled for the floatation devices. "For if we meet again, I shan't be so kind." Carter turned back to the crew. They all looked to him and, Carter realized, waited.

They waited for orders.

He tried to catch Brad's eye, but his big brother did not look away from the floundering pirates below. His face was wrought with worry.

So he turned to Yvette. "Fill our sails, matey. Let's put some distance between us and these filthy smears on the pirate code."

"Aye, sir," Yvette answered. She called out commands to the others.

The crew bustled about the deck, unfurling sails, untying lines, hoisting anchor.

And they were away.

11

A drift in a sea of hatred, caught in a riptide of loathing and humiliation, drifted two pirates, although calling them pirates was a stretch. They honored no code and sailed under no banner. They served no greater purpose, sought no grand adventure that didn't line their pockets. Indeed, they'd sooner avoid the adventure and jump straight to the treasure. But, sail these seas long enough and, no matter how hard you may try to avoid it, sooner or later adventure will find you. And find them it did.

Kids!

Sunk by a bunch of kids. Some wannabes who'd seen too many movies. Had no idea what being a pirate really was. They still thought it was all about treasure and adventure and having a merry old time sailing the seven seas. Singing shanties and doing stupid little dances as they swabbed the deck.

They'd never seen behind the silver screen. They'd never seen what *real* pirates do. No, they wouldn't have the stomach for that.

Kids!

"What's the plan, Nestor?" JJ asked as he floundered like a fish. "We swimming for shore?"

Not bloody likely. There was no turning back for Nestor. He couldn't let this slight stand. He couldn't let that snot nosed brat of a kid get away with putting him in the drink.

The kid caught him off guard is all. Who would have thought some prepubescent know-it-all would have the stones to put a hole in the side of a boat like that? The kid was nuts, plain and simple. No way could Nestor have planned for that.

"No," Nestor answered. "We are *not* swimming back to shore. This is a high traffic area. Someone will be along sooner or later."

"Before my legs cramp, and I drown?" JJ wondered aloud.

"Better hope so," Nestor answered, venom in his tone.

They'd been treading water for close to an hour, but the pain in Nestor's legs hadn't even registered in his brain. His mind was too crowded with thoughts of revenge. Of all the things he'd do to that kid once he found him.

You wanna play at being a pirate, kid? No problem. I'll happily show you some of the torture methods they were famous for.

Somewhere among the shouting voices in Nestor's head was a little one, barely heard above the others. A squeaky voice, like that of a church mouse or a whiny kid with teary eyes and a bruised cheek. A voice from long, long ago.

Nestor tried to ignore it, but it wouldn't stop whining. "The big kids took my book," it cried. "My favorite book about Calico Jack Rackham."

And a deep, slurred voice answered, "So what? What's a book good for anyway? It pay the bills?" And the man who spoke with the deep voice shoved the whiny kid away and turned up the television.

Nestor slapped the water like he was trying to shoo the memory away, and he splashed salt in its eye.

Moments later, Nestor heard the faint whirring of an engine. He turned toward it to see a modest, aging fishing boat bouncing over the waves.

"See?" he said to JJ, who was seconds away from sinking. "Told you someone would come along."

They waved their arms in the air and shouted for help. The fishing boat changed course and headed to their rescue. The two grizzled men aboard tossed Nestor and JJ a line and pulled them close to the hull. Then they leaned over and hauled the two men out of the water.

"What the heck are you guys doing out here without a boat?" one of the men asked. He was older, grandfatherly. "Y'all tourists or something? Get sucked out here by a riptide? No matter. I ain't one to judge. Especially if a person is in trouble."

The other man handed Nestor and JJ towels and draped a couple blankets over a railing for them to use when they were ready. The other man was younger, maybe the older one's son. A family business, this must have been. How quaint.

That whiny little voice started crying again. Wailed as his father slapped a book out of his hand. "Told you, books ain't good for nothing. You want to be useful, get a job, pay some bills, stop crying all the time."

The little boy swallowed the anguish and wiped away the tears.

"Just like your mother," the father said. "All she ever did was cry. 'Til she up and took off. Worthless, the both of you."

The father was a fisherman. Not a very good one. His hands were rarely steady enough to steer his ship toward anything resembling a bounty. It was questionable whether the rusty, old boat would get them where they were going, anyway. But, even so, the boy dreamed of sailing the decrepit ship alongside his cuss of a father. Didn't matter how often he imagined the both of them on the bottom of the sea.

Maybe that's where the father and that boat were. They both took off one day and never came back, leaving that boy alone with nothing but his books. But, like the father said, books don't pay the bills or put food in your belly.

Nestor dried his face, and spoke through the towel. "We did have a boat. It sunk."

"What the heck from?" the older man said, surprised. "No storms recently. And nothing to run into. We're in open water."

Nestor dropped the towel to reveal the nasty smile on his face, the kind of smile that immediately puts another on guard. The kind of smile full of malice and ill intent. "Pirates," he said.

The younger man scoffed. "Right. I suppose they put a cannonball through your hull?"

"Matter-of-fact," JJ said. He'd slipped behind the younger man without him noticing. JJ grabbed his wrists and pinned his arms behind his back. "That's just about right."

Nestor stepped to the older man, jutted his chin up, and stared through large, wild eyes. "And now we find ourselves in need of a new vessel."

64

The fishermen didn't put up a fight. They were both tired, probably been out at sea all day. Nestor and JJ tied them up with a length of rope they found in the cabin, tight knots binding their wrists and ankles, and gagged them with rags.

"So, what now?" JJ asked as Nestor acquainted himself with the helm.

"Drop these two at the nearest port, and then track down those kids. I watched where they went. Straight for the Bahamas."

"Why?" JJ asked. "They don't have anything we want. No money. We can snag another boat like that somewhere else."

Nestor shot JJ a glare like a rusty cutlass. "For what they did. They sunk us. Put us in the water. Our code demands we seek retribution."

"We have a code?" JJ seemed dumbfounded.

Nestor grabbed JJ by the collar. Then he reached into his own collar and pulled out one of the gold chains hanging around his neck. Dangling from it was a skull and crossbones pendant.

"No retreat, no surrender, no mercy," Nestor recited. "*That* is our code, and I take it very seriously."

JJ straightened his collar and laughed uncomfortably. "Right, that code. I know that code. I thought you meant some other code."

Nestor pushed the throttle and steered toward the kids' path. "We're the last of a breed. It's time we acted like it. So, you're either with me." He pointed overboard. "Or you're back with the fishes."

"Yo-ho," JJ said, unenthusiastically.

They sailed on slowly as the night waned and the sun peeked over the horizon. The crew hadn't gotten much sleep, but the adrenaline hadn't left their systems yet. They hadn't even fully comprehended that they just faced down armed gunmen.

Really. Who does that?

If at no other point during their adventure so far, it was then that Carter realized this was not a game. He never really did anyway. This was always the real deal. The way out. The way to stay together.

Freedom.

But he saw the change that realization brought about in the others. He worried that it would scare them off, send them paddling back home to welcome the shackles of curfews and chore lists for fear of the unknown that lay ahead. Instead, they embraced it.

Louis, who had disappeared below deck an hour earlier, emerged behind an armload of color clothing and accessories. "Raided the closets downstairs. Found some great stuff."

"For what?" Marcus said. "Dressing up like a rich old lady?"

"Proper pirate garb," Louis said. "We need to look the part." He spread the clothes out on the deck—silk shirts, scarves, gaudy necklaces, bandanas. They cut ribbons out of dresses and tied them around their arms and legs. Tied bandanas and scarves around their heads. Loaded their wrists with gold and silver bangles.

Once finished, they looked like a proper pirate crew. Sort of.

They stood in a circle, admiring each other. Bit by bit, they were becoming more along the lines of what Carter had envisioned. This whole thing was becoming what he always wanted. Adventure, freedom, life on the high seas.

"Perfect," Carter said. "This is a scurvy bunch of sea dogs if ever I've seen one. We're ready to sail for treasure now."

"No, we aren't," Brad said in his stern, wannabe parent voice. "Not by a longshot." He was holding his keychain again, that cheap bauble he always kept close.

Carter took a deep breath, tried to remain calm, tried to not let Brad's naysaying bring him down.

"We're not going anywhere... Until we decide on a captain."

Carter's stomach sank. He knew it was coming. He knew Brad would try to take charge, make rules, give them curfew, take them back home if things got out of hand. Armed gunmen probably classified as out of hand.

Carter sighed. If he had to be a deckhand to continue this adventure, then he would. He didn't need to be captain. Even though that's all he ever dreamed about. But if taking a step back for them to move forward was required, he could live with it.

Sort of.

"So let's take a vote," Yvette said.

Brad stepped in before anyone could speak. "I just want to say something first."

A collective groan came from Louis, Marcus, and Yvette.

"This is a democracy, right?" Brad asked the group.

They consented and gestured for Brad to continue.

"I think you all know that I thought this was a bad idea from the start," Brad said. "Like, really bad. Maybe the worst. Anyway, I was dead against it. And, despite how much fun you might be having, you can't deny that I was right, at least a little, to question this." He pointed at the horizon behind him. "I mean, we almost just became a Lifetime Original Movie—*Orphans Kidnapped by Pirates*. Or worse, a headline—*Flesh Picked from Orphans' Bones after Being Totally Shot to Pieces by Spray Tan Pirates*."

The others didn't laugh. That's okay, Brad thought. He wasn't trying to be funny.

Brad paced the deck, looking in each of their eyes. All but Carter's. "That stuff just can't happen anymore. If we're going to continue on with this, we need to be safe about it. No more *playing* pirates. If we keep going, we *are* pirates. And pirates aren't fools."

Finally, he looked at Carter, and Carter saw something he did not expect.

A smile.

Brad continued. "Pirates were tacticians. Smart. Tricky. They were the Navy SEALs of their day. They knew when to fight, they knew when to hide. But, most of all, they were adventurous. They were brave. That's who we need to serve as our captain." He turned away from Carter and addressed the crew. "And I think it's obvious who that needs to be." Brad puffed out his chest, stood tall, and looked squarely at his little brother. "I nominate Carter as captain."

Wait, what? Carter couldn't believe his ears.

"Gasp," Louis said. "Plot twist."

"I second that," Darla said.

"I third it," said Yvette. "Is that even a thing, *thirding* it?"

"I don't think so," Louis said. "But it sounds cool."

Marcus stood. "I object."

"Double gasp," Louis said. "Plot twist again."

Marcus shook his head and frowned, like he'd bitten into an apple and saw only half a worm. "If I'm gonna put my trust in you to get us to some treasure and not get eaten by sharks or shot by spray-tans, you gotta have a better name than Captain Carter. It's lame, bro. And I won't follow a lame captain."

Silence. The wheels of everyone's mind began turning, some faster than others.

"*El azote de los mares*," Yvette said after a few moments. "It means, 'the scourge of the seas.'"

"Not bad," said Louis. "A little aggressive, perhaps, but still, not bad."

"What about, Captain Kickin' Butts and Takin' Names," Marcus posed.

He found himself on the receiving end of everyone's stare.

"What? It was just a thought. Jeez. Y'all are lame," Marcus added.

"I've got it," said Louis. "Captain Cartier, the Prince of the Pacific."

Marcus scoffed. "You should be chucked overboard just for *thinking* that, let alone actually saying it. And for your information, we're in the *Atlantic,* not the Pacific."

"I know, but Pacific had a nicer ring to it."

"No. *Hell no!*" Marcus said. "No way I'm taking orders from a captain named after a jewelry designer."

"Wow! Marcus, I'm impressed," Louis said appreciatively.

"Just because I can't afford bling doesn't mean I don't know who makes it," Marcus retorted. "You of all people, Louis. That's very narrow-minded."

"Point taken."

Everyone was silent for another minute or so, nobody wanting to give voice to a name that was silly, or lame, or just plain dumb.

Suddenly, Brad smiled and nodded his head. He walked over to Carter and put his hands on Carter's smooth, soft cheeks. "Lackbeard."

"Ooh, that's good," said Louis. "Really good. I'm jealous I didn't think of it."

Darla lit up like a Roman candle. "I love it."

"Perfecto," said Yvette.

Marcus nodded. "When you're right, you're right."

In his best grizzled pirate voice, Brad said it again. "Lackbeard."

Hmm, it does have a pretty cool ring to it, Carter thought.

"All in favor?" Darla said.

"Aye," the crew said in unison.

Carter stared at his brother for the longest of moments before turning away, pretending to have something in his eye. *Pirate captains don't cry!* He brushed away the imaginary dirt and addressed his crew. "Thank you." His voice cracked. He tried to cover it up by clearing his throat and speaking in his pirate voice. "We've won our first battle, but I assure ye, it won't be the last. The sea, she's unforgiving. She cares not for our plights or dreams of treasure and freedom. She will pull us down to her murky depths first chance she gets. To say nothing of the salty dogs who sail atop her." He untied his skull and crossbones bandana from his head and handed it to Yvette. "But I promise, with every ounce of salt in my blood, that I will get us to the 'x' on that map, and to all the dreams that await us there."

A round of cheers sounded from the crew as Yvette ran the skull and crossbones up the mast.

Brad clapped his hand on Carter's shoulder. "Well, Captain Lackbeard, what are your orders?"

"Set course for Eleuthera, and make haste!" Lackbeard yelled. "There's coin to be had."

13

The sea air tasted saltier than the bottom of a bag of pretzels as the midday sun beat down on Carter. It was like a meal, finely seasoned. The sweet wind was his dessert. Everything seemed brighter and better now that he was officially captain. But, for some reason, he couldn't stop staring at his reflection on the surface of the water and thinking about land. Or, if he was honest, the people on that land. And the people buried in that land.

"Course is set, Captain," Brad said as he approached the bow where Carter sat. "Darla, Yvette and I found some old maps and stuff. Plus, this boat has a GPS. Eleuthera isn't that far. Did you know that the Bahamas is only fifty miles from where we live? Paradise, so close to the dump we grew up in."

Carter didn't turn away from the water. Brad must have noticed the slump in his shoulders.

"What's wrong?"

Carter shrugged. "I don't know."

Brad sat down next to him, let his legs dangle over the edge. He looked down, and now the distorted reflections of both Humbolt brothers stared back at them.

The silence stretched from the bow to the horizon.

"I was scared," Brad finally said. "When those guys pulled those guns out, I totally froze. My mind went blank. All I could think of was the barrel of that gun." Brad paused, gave Carter a chance to speak. When he didn't, Brad continued. "Then I thought of you and Darla. I wanted to protect you, but I didn't know what to do. Ever since, I've just felt embarrassed. Ashamed, maybe. I'm supposed to protect you. That's my job."

Silence again. The rest of the crew sounded far away, like their voices carried across the water all the way from home.

"You ever think about Mom?" Carter finally asked, breaking the silence.

The question caught Brad by surprise. He sat for a long moment before answering. "Yeah. A lot. You?"

Carter was barely three when their mother had died. He didn't have many memories of her. The picture of her that he had in his head was like a reflection seen from the corner of his eye. It shifted, changed, sometimes looked a little too much like the mom on whatever movie he'd last seen.

"Yeah," Carter answered. He suddenly felt the pressing urge to change the subject. So he plucked the first thing that came to his mind and spit it out. "I miss Linn, too."

His cheeks turned a bright shade of red, and he immediately wished he'd plucked something else. "You know, because she was such a good friend and stuff." Carter floundered to rebound from the shock of his own words. "And if it wasn't for her, we wouldn't have gotten away from the orphanage. She sacrificed herself. Like Gandalf."

Brad laughed and seemed generous enough to let the subject drop. "Yeah, well, Gandalf comes back after that. And more powerful, too. I'll bet you'll see Linn again. You know, as a friend." Maybe he wasn't feeling that generous.

"Hey, guys!" Yvette yelled. "I think we might have a problem."

Everyone rushed to her at the helm.

"What's wrong?" Brad asked.

She pointed up at the sky. "That."

A fat, black cloud sat between them and Eleuthera. Judging size and distance out on the open sea could be a challenge, but this thing seemed like a black hole had opened up in the sky. And black holes swallowed everything that came near them. But they didn't have a choice. It was far too big to go around. The only way was through.

"Captain?" Yvette said.

"Batten down the hatches," he said. "It's rough seas ahead."

"You think?" Marcus said, rolling his eyes. "Instead of Captain Lackbeard, maybe we should call you Captain Obvious."

Carter gave his friend a cross look. "Now's not the time, rapscallion."

Marcus shook his head. "A'ight, Captain. I'm a gettin'."

As the crew ran about, removing everything from the deck that could go overboard and bringing it below, tying down whatever could be tied down, Carter noticed Yvette's eyes still fixed on the storm cloud. There was something odd about them, a shade he'd never noticed before: fear.

He stood beside her, still at the helm. He leaned in close and whispered in his normal voice, "Yvette, are you okay?"

She sucked in a quick breath, startled. "Fine."

If there was one thing Carter knew about Yvette, it was that she was tough as nails. And even when she wasn't, she was. At least, that's what she wanted everyone to think. That she was always strong, never afraid, had nerves of steel, and never backed down. But even in the foster care system, where kids are constantly putting up fronts, where you can peel away layers for years before you see a kid for who they actually are, live with a person long enough and you get glimpses of their true selves.

Carter had caught a few glimpses of Yvette over the years. He would never tell her that because she would probably punch him. But he'd seen through the cracks in her armor. He saw it when they first stepped on the boat—a little hesitation, a slight tremble. Before she took a deep breath and quickly spackled over those cracks.

She came to the United States like many Cubans— on a rickety boat that was barely seaworthy, with her family. She arrived in America an orphan.

"You sure?" Carter asked. "Because we could totally—"

"I said I'm fine," she said, her voice unwavering.

Carter nodded, and then joined the others in securing the boat. With the hustle and bustle, he'd almost forgotten why they were rushing to tie everything down. Until thunder rolled across the water and lightning pierced the sky in the distance.

"She's comin' on us," Carter said to the crew. "What

say we hit this beast head on, run her through and make landfall in time for supper?"

A rowdy cheer erupted from the crew.

But one remained silent.

"Helmsman," Carter said. "Take us through."

Yvette didn't move. Sweat beaded on her brow.

Carter repeated his orders.

"No," Yvette said.

A gasp from the crew.

Carter marched up to her, to remind her that she'd signed the articles and took an oath to obey her captain. But when he saw her chin quivering, he softened his approach. "Yvette, I know this is hard for you, so if you want someone else to—"

"That's not what this is about," she said, clenching her jaw. "This is about me knowing what I'm doing. My parents taught me everything they knew about sailing. And we are *not* sailing into that storm."

Carter studied her face, then those of the crew, and then he looked to the storm. A firm hand on his shoulder turned him around.

"Part of being a good captain," Brad said, "is knowing when to trust your crew."

Carter looked back at the storm. His dreams lay just on the other side. So close he felt like he could reach out and grab them. He could practically smell the treasure on the wind.

Was that determination on Yvette's face or just a mask of fear? Did she want to run?

No. Yvette didn't run from anything.

"Okay, helmsman, then what do you propose?"

Yvette pointed up at the storm clouds, defiant, like she was cursing the dreaded things. "If we charge through and get too close to land, we won't have any room to maneuver, and we risk being smashed against the shore."

"I vote no smashing," Louis said.

"Second," Marcus quickly added.

"What are our options?" Carter asked.

"We could try to outrun it," Yvette said, pointing behind them. "Haul it back toward Florida, and we might make it before the storm reaches us."

Carter's chin dug into his chest. The very thing he did not want to hear. She did want to run. Wanted to sail back to the safety of dry land and locked doors and storm windows.

"Or," she said.

And Carter's heart leapt.

"We could heave-to."

Louis raised his hand. "I'm glad you said that because I think I just heave-to'd in my mouth a little."

Yvette smacked Louis in the shoulder. "Keep it in your guts." Then to Carter: "Not many people know how to heave-to anymore. Most just run and try to sail through. But my parents showed me. It's basically parking in open water and weathering the storm. We trim the jib aback, trim the main in hard, and lash the helm."

"Yeah, what she said," Marcus stated, clueless.

"You really think it's our best play?" Carter asked.

Yvette nodded. "I do. I mean... Aye, Captain!"

"Then let's do it," Carter said. "Tell us what to do."

Yvette barked out orders, and the crew hurried about, tying off lines and trimming sails. The wind began to howl. Rain fell. "We're good," she said to the crew after the work was done. "Now we head below and hunker down. It's about to get rocky."

The crew needed no more urging. They hurried below deck.

Carter paused when he noticed that Yvette wasn't following. "You said we're good, right?"

"Yeah," she answered, but she sounded far away. She craned her head all the way back, stared straight up at the sky and let the rain fall on her face. She jumped when the lightning flashed and the thunder roared, but she didn't leave the helm.

Carter walked back to her side.

"I have this exact same nightmare every night," she said. "On a boat, at sea, in the middle of a storm. Just me and my family. A wave slams our starboard. Everyone screams. My mom's hand slips through my fingers. Then I wake up, and my family is gone."

Carter grabbed Yvette's hand. "This family will still be here when you wake up."

Her face was wet with rain and tears. She brushed it all away. She smiled and nodded. Then the two of them went below with the rest.

They were all huddled together on the bed, arms and legs weaving together into one trembling human tapestry. They opened up and absorbed Carter and Yvette, and became a singular blanket that kept them all warm through the night.

Carter dozed off a few times despite the often violent rocking of the boat. He woke when each crack of thunder made the crew shriek in unison. He never let go of Yvette's hand, though. Or maybe she never let go of his.

Eventually, the rocking slowed, the thunder faded, and the sun pierced the clouds. Carter slipped Louis's hand into Yvette's, and unwove himself from the tapestry. He made his way topside to survey the damage only to find Brad doing the same.

"How's it looking?" Carter asked.

"Pretty good, from what I can tell," Brad said. "Yvette would know better." He poked at the GPS on the console. "Doesn't look like we've been blown too much off course. Eleuthera is still only an hour away, give or take."

Carter wiped the water off the vinyl seat and sat, his butt still getting wet. Words formed in his mouth, but dissolved on his tongue before he could say them. Finally, he said the only two words that didn't fall apart. "Thanks, bro."

"Just reading what's on the GPS," Brad said with a shrug.

"No, I mean, for everything." Carter fumbled with words again before deciding to just let them go. "For backing me as captain. I know you didn't have to do that. You could have made yourself captain, and everyone would have listened to you. You could have taken us back. And for reminding me to listen to Yvette last night. I would have tried to ram through that storm."

Brad smiled, shoved Carter over, and squeezed next to him in the seat. They stared ahead, at the horizon. "Look, I know that you think I worry too much or that I'm a stick in the mud or whatever. One of us has to be sometimes. But I don't want to be all the time. Truth is, I want this adventure just as much as you. I need it. And I couldn't have it if I was leading. I don't want to lead this one. Plus, you're good at it, Carter. That thing with those pirates was awesome. You fought off actual pirates. You're a beast!"

Brad slid so he faced Carter. "So, I'll make a deal with you. As long as you keep leading like you are, I'm totally cool with following. But if things start going off the rails, I'm pulling the plug."

Carter turned to meet him. "If I'm going to keep leading as captain, then I'll need a good first mate at my side." He extended his hand. "Deal?"

Brad took it, and they shook. "Deal."

Carter sat back and stretched his arms through a big yawn. "Good. Then first order of business. Wake up Louis so he can make breakfast. And second order, let's get back on course. We're landing on Eleuthera today."

14

Meanwhile, in the ramshackle home of a legendary fisherman, as a new trophy was mounted, the amazing exploits of Captain Lackbeard began to spread.

Walter hoisted the rear axle of a Chevy Suburban onto the hooks screwed into his wall. His biggest catch to date. And shiniest. He still couldn't piece together what an SUV would want with a hunk of beef, but who knew what those newfangled cars did these days. Heck, a neighbor up the street had one that ran on corn. *Corn!* Maybe this one ran on red meat.

Either way, it was his now. A hard fought victory that needed to be celebrated. And it was definitely hard fought. His arms would ache for days from reeling that sucker in.

As he set it and fiddled with it until it was just right, a breaking news report interrupted his regularly scheduled programming. *Rats!* Now he'd never know if Dante was actually Ned's twin brother who had plastic surgery in Brazil and returned to take over the family business.

"The investigation continues into the disappearance

of six teens and preteens from the St. John's County Children's Orphanage," the newscaster said.

Walter whipped around to see footage of the house next door. "Holy Moses," he whispered.

The newscaster continued. "After an apparent altercation with a representative from the Valley Forge Military Academy, in which a Chevy Suburban was destroyed, but none were hurt, police believe the children stole a van belonging to the orphanage and made their way here to the Cove Marina on Camachee Island, where they stole a sailboat. Police now believe the children are at sea and possibly in danger. Stay tuned for further details."

Regularly scheduled programming continued. Dante really is Ned's disguised twin brother!

Walter shut the TV off. He walked outside, onto his porch, and stared at the orphanage. Such a nuisance that place was. Kids always running through his yard, stealing his fishing poles on some sort of dare. They made up stories about him, and laughed as they walked by his house.

He marched next door when he saw the woman who ran the place follow some musclebound Sly Stallone wannabe out the front door.

"Roberts," Walter called. "Hey, Roberts," he called again when she didn't answer.

Ms. Roberts spun on her heel and leveled a finger like a gun barrel at his chest. "What is it, you crazy old man?"

"Which kids went missing?"

The walking pectorals stepped toward Walter. "What concern is that of yours, sir?"

Walter looked the man up and down. "Who's talking to you, Rambo?" As he stared the man in the eye,

Walter remembered the mention of a military academy on the news, and something about a destroyed SUV. He turned to Ms. Roberts before the military man could respond. "Darla with them?"

"Like my friend said," Ms. Roberts answered as she ran a hand over Rambo's arm. "What's it to you?"

"Darla Roberts is believed to be with them, yes," Rambo said. "If you have any information regarding their whereabouts, it is your patriotic duty to tell me this instant."

Walter snorted and walked back to his house.

"Don't mind him," he heard Ms. Roberts say. "Just a crazy old man."

Darla was the only one in that entire house who treated Walter like a person instead of some neighborhood ghost story or charity case. The house and everyone in it could wash into the sea for all he cared. But not her.

And her own mother looked like she could give a crap. More focused on Corporal Bench Press. Well, Walter would not stand for that. He would not let Darla be forgotten, because she would not let him be forgotten.

He filled a pack with supplies—shark hooks, his best lures, plenty of line. Then he grabbed his best pole and a harpoon gun and walked outside. He stood in his driveway, looking at the dirty tarp for several minutes. It was fraying along its edges. Full of holes. It hadn't been moved in years. Since the last time Walter took her out.

That was *not* a good day at sea.

Heck, who was he kidding? That was a *bad* day.

Very bad.

He took a step back. Thought about just going back in the house, turning the TV on. He wanted to. What had Dante been doing in Brazil all those years? But he didn't. Darla needed him. And the sea was calling his name once again.

He ripped the tarp away.

There she was. The *Salty Walty* in all her glory. Granted, she'd seen better days. Most of her paint was peeling. She was warped in places. Was that a hole in the hull? Might be a hole. But she'd still sail just fine.

"Whatd'ya say, old girl?" Walter asked as her ran his hand along the old barnacle-encrusted hull, filling his palm with shell fragments and splinters. "You got one more ride left in ya?"

15

"Land ho!"

More welcome words had never reached Captain Lackbeard's ears. Marcus yelled it again. "Land ho!" And a wave of cheers erupted from the crew

"Take us in, helmsman," Carter said to Yvette.

She scanned the GPS and then the shoreline. "Looks like there's a cove up that way a bit. We could drop anchor there."

"Then make it so," the captain ordered.

The boat jostled over the waves, which grew choppier the closer they got to shore. But each member of the crew was glued to the bow, awed at the sight of the island. They'd done it. They'd really done it. Commandeered a ship. Set sail. Fought off pirates. Weathered a storm. And, now, reached a treasure island.

As they stared at the island, Carter stared at them. His crew.

The boat rounded a bend in the shore, and a gorgeous cove opened up before them. The water was the kind of blue you see in brochures, and clear enough that you could see the schools of fish sunning as the water grew shallow. The beach was lined with palm trees.

They had found paradise.

The boat slowed. "Dropping anchor," Yvette called. And they stopped thirty feet from shore.

Silence but for the lapping of waves.

It had been only a day since they set sail, but, for Carter, this was a journey that began years ago, when his mom gave him a Teddy bear with a pirate eyepatch, and then was gone. The day they lost her—that was the day he set sail.

"Well, Captain," Brad said, "we've arrived. And I'm sure you're anxious to find some treasure, but if I may speak for the crew, I think some R&R is in order."

Carter looked at their faces and knew Brad was right. And, truthfully, Carter wasn't as anxious to find treasure as Brad probably thought. Finding the treasure meant the hunt was over. And hunting treasure was as far as Carter's plan stretched. What came after was whatever came after.

Choosing to show his answer instead of say it, Carter whipped of his shirt and jumped off the boat, smacking the surface of the water with the best cannonball of his life. The others followed suit. Geysers shot into the air as a hail of bodies hit the water.

Carter dove down until he touched the bottom. He grabbed a fistful of sand before bobbing back to the surface. As he treaded water, he let the sand slip through his fingers and sink back to the ocean floor.

And then a burst of water splashed in his face. He spit the salt water from his mouth and wiped it from his eyes to see Darla swimming away from him, laughing like a mermaid. Carter shot through the water like a dolphin after her. He caught her ankle, dunked her, only to be dunked by Marcus.

The crew once again became one big intertwined mass. But this time they did not come together for collective security, to soothe one another. They laughed and whooped and hollered until their lungs, half-full of sea water, ached, and their bellies, starting to grumble, grew tired.

The orphanage was less than a mile from a small, public beach. They took a day trip there once, but when Ms. Roberts wandered off, hot on the trail of some young lifeguard, and Brad had to pull one of the younger kids out of a rip tide, they never went back.

And noise was strongly discouraged. Which meant no loud laughter, no horseplay, very little play at all, actually, when Ms. Roberts was near.

This was one of the very few times when Carter could recall playing openly and loudly with others without fear of being smacked on the back of the head by his caretaker. One of the very few times when he felt like a normal kid.

As the crew grew tired of treading water, they moved closer to shore, into the shallows. And, soon, they were on the beach. Brad and Darla laid outstretched, the tips of their fingers just barely touching. Yvette sat with her feet in the water, staring out at the waves. Marcus and Louis explored a rocky outcrop a bit further down the beach.

Carter waded in the shallows, sat on his butt so the water came up to his chest, and dug his hands into the sand.

"What are you going to do with your share of the treasure?" Darla asked to no one in particular.

"Go to cooking school," Louis shouted from atop a craggy rock. "And then open my own restaurant."

"Buy the Pittsburgh Pirates," Marcus said.

"Sail around the world," Yvette said. "In my own yacht."

"I would travel," Darla said as she looked up at the sky. "I'd go everywhere. And I wouldn't stop until I'd seen everything." She looked at Brad. "What about you?"

Brad didn't answer at first. He just squinted into the sun. "I don't know. Nothing exciting, really. I'd just... you know, be normal."

Carter sunk deeper into the water. He was up to his chin now.

"We're dreaming here," Darla said. "And that's what you come up with? Be normal?"

Brad shifted on the sand. "Yeah. Normal's something I've never had."

The water rushed up over Carter's head as he lay back. The conversation was gone. All he could hear was the sea and the blood in his ears. He closed his eyes, and was alone.

When his lungs started to burn and beg for oxygen, he stayed under a little longer. Then he broke the surface and took in the sweet tropical air.

He called to the crew. "I'm hungry. Who's hungry?"

Everyone answered in the affirmative. Marcus did so in true dramatic fashion, doubling over and pretending that his stomach had started to eat itself. They all swam back to the boat.

Carter was happy on the beach, but he felt at home the moment his feet touched the boat's deck.

Louis disappeared below to prepare lunch while the

rest dried off in the sun. Marcus fell asleep. Yvette lay on the bow and let her feet hang over the edge. Brad and Darla snuggled up on the bench seats. No one said anything. Not until after they ate.

"All right," Marcus said through a yawn and mouthful of grilled cheese sandwich. "I'm rested. I'm fed. I'm ready to get off this boat and find our fortune."

"Most of the day is already gone," Darla said. "It's not a good idea to set off now and explore with sunset so close."

Carter had thought the same thing, but he was glad he didn't have to say it. A pirate captain couldn't show fear. Of anything.

"I know," Marcus said. "But I want to sleep on solid ground. Let's camp out on the beach."

The crew swelled with excitement at the idea. They looked to Carter.

"Captain?" Brad asked.

Carter nodded. "Let's do it. Pack up everything we'll need for the night and tomorrow. We'll set off first thing in the morning."

They loaded an inflatable raft they'd found below deck with all of the supplies, and then made their way to shore. They built a fire, dreamed more about what they'd do with the treasure, made dinner, and fell asleep.

Carter stayed up, looking at the stars. He'd never seen so many, and so bright. He was so distracted by their beauty that he didn't hear Brad walk up behind him.

"Can't sleep?" Brad asked.

"Haven't tried," Carter answered.

Brad sat down beside him. "So what's going on with you?"

"What do you mean?"

"I mean, you've been sad-sacking all over the place since we got here."

Carter felt a surge of guilt—over something he couldn't quite define. He knew he felt guilty. And he sort of knew why. But something about it eluded him. Something that he couldn't put into words.

"Listening to you all talk about what you'd do with the treasure." Carter drew circles in the sand with his finger. He watched the pattern deepen instead of look at his brother. "I don't know. It just, I guess, made me realize that I hadn't thought that far ahead."

That was a practice that Carter had honed over the years—not thinking ahead, just living in the moment. Because that was all he could count on. Dreaming of the future was dangerous when you were in the foster care system. You never knew when your entire life might change. Someone could come and adopt you, but not your brother. Or your brother and not you. Either way, you're separated.

And if you find yourself taken in by a foster family, you never know if they'll change their mind or get sick of you in a few days, weeks, years and send you back. Like a bad meal at a restaurant.

"Earlier, when you and Darla were talking... What did you mean by 'normal'?" Carter asked.

Brad shrugged. "Going to college. Buying a house. Starting a family. Stuff like that."

"I never knew you thought about those things," Carter said.

"Yeah, sometimes. Or only when treasure hunting, I guess. When I actually have a shot at making it happen. It's just a fantasy."

Carter still did not look up from the sand. He dug his finger in deeper. "I guess." They were all just fantasies. But they were fantasies that took them all to different places. If Carter was honest, if he had one fantasy about what he would do with the treasure, it would be to hunt more treasure. He would keep doing exactly what he was doing, with the same exact people.

"I guess it just surprised me," Carter with a smile.

"Surprised me a little, too," Brad said. He nudged Carter, and then stood. "Come on, let's get some sleep. Need to be rested for the trek tomorrow. Who knows what we're going to find on this island?"

Carter watched as the water rolled up the beach and filled the little trench he'd dug with his finger. As the water washed back out to sea, he let it carry his worry out with it. He felt another surge of guilt, but this time at his own childishness. He was living his dream right now, but instead of enjoying it, he was sulking.

No more. Pirates don't sulk.

He stood up. "So many booby traps, I bet. It's gonna be awesome."

16

Sweat soaked Carter's shirt to his back. He'd risen long before the sun with a fresh perspective and vigor, ready to find the treasure of Eleuthera. The crew rose when that vigor came howling out of his lungs.

"On yer feet, scallywags!" he shouted.

They all shot up from the sand. Brad tripped over himself and fell flat on his face. Louis ran around screaming about scorpions until Yvette smacked him across the face, snapping him out of his tizzy.

"Thanks, I needed that," Louis said, not really meaning it.

"It's four in the morning," Brad grumbled.

"Never too early when there's treasure to be found," Carter said, ignoring the eye-daggers being hurled at him. "You think treasure cares what time it is?"

Not a single reply came.

"Okay then. Let's rock 'n roll!"

Not a pleasant look passed between them as they broke camp. Except from Louis. He passed out some ration kits he'd assembled, and seemed absolutely delighted to do so. The glassy looks and hoarse grumbles didn't dampen his shine.

Only Carter acknowledged the glee and matched it in equal measure. "Holy crap, man. This look amazing!"

"Thanks, Captain. This sort of stuff is my forte. I've been good at it since I was a kid." Louis's eyes sparkled. "I used to make these when Lord and Lady Fluffington, my stuffed bears, would host their semi-regular galas. I made one for my dad once, too." The sparkle in his eyes suddenly dimmed. "He wasn't as appreciative as the Fluffingtons."

Louis was one of the few from the home whose parents were actually alive. Carter used to be jealous of that. But he realized recently that it may have been worse for Louis—to have parents who didn't want him.

"The Fluffingtons sound like they have impeccable taste," Carter said, and the sparkle returned somewhat to Louis's eyes.

Once the crew was ready and mostly awake, they marched into the jungle, the pale light of morning still hours off.

"We should have waited for sun up," Brad said as he struggled through a thicket of vines.

"Nonsense," Carter said. "Now we'll reach the treasure before the heat of the day."

"This island is a lot bigger than that map suggests," Louis said. His typically chalky face was beet red. "You sure that thing's drawn to scale?"

"No, I'm not," Carter said. "In fact, I'm quite certain that it's not to scale at all."

Darla held up her iPad. "But satellite imagery and GPS don't lie. I spent most of the boat trip comparing this map to aerial photos of the island. I can get us there. We should actually be pretty close. It's just on the other side of this…" Her voice sank into an endless swamp, a muck-filled bog that stretched on endlessly. "Of this," she said, defeated.

"Well, I guess we're getting gross," Carter said as he hiked up his pants.

"Whoa, whoa," Louis said, throwing up his hands. "Louis doesn't do gross. Certainly not bottomless bogs of gross that are probably stupid with leeches."

"Is there any other way?" Carter asked.

Darla tapped on the tablet, compared it to the map. "Yeah, I think so. But we'd need to cross what appears to be a pretty massive chasm."

Louis seemed to shrink. "Louis doesn't do chasms either."

"You're afraid of heights?" Marcus asked.

"Afraid? Not at all," Louis replied. "I'm freakin' terrified!"

"Well, Louis better make up his mind. Gross or… freakin' terrified," Marcus mimicked in a high-pitched squeal that drew giggles from some of the others.

Louis stared at the bog. His face crinkled at the sight and smell of it. But Carter could see him almost throw up in his mouth at the thought of looking over the edge of a chasm. "Gross it is."

Slowly, as if trying not to disturb what might be living inside, the crew waded into the bog. Squeals of unease emanated from Louis the moment his feet touched the muck. He was a tea kettle.

Marcus hurried across, pushing through the swamp like it was a pool of acid.

No one spoke. They all tensed, probably hoping that if they stayed as quiet as possible, they could pretend their pants weren't filling with muck.

Carter broke the silence, and the crew's hard-faked peace of mind. "Anyone else feel like they're in a horror movie?"

The crew groaned.

"Don't," Marcus snapped. "Do. Not. Go. There. I'm the only brown kid here. If this thing turns from adventure to horror, the brown kid *always* gets screwed."

They reached the other side without another word. They all climbed onto the far bank and twitched as shivers ran up and down their spines.

Carter moved to continue their quest, but something didn't feel right. Like maybe it wasn't only shivers running up and down his body. "Anyone else feel...?"

"Yeah," Brad said before Carter could finish. "Something weird."

"Don't," Louis said. "Just don't even. I don't want to know. Because if it's leeches, I'm gonna die."

"Um, what?" Darla blurted.

Carter adjusted his headlamp, and shined it at the crew. There were black blobs all over their bodies.

Louis started jumping up and down, shaking his arms like he was trying to fly away. "I knew it! I knew I didn't want to know. Gross, gross, gross! I'm gonna die, I'm gonna die!"

Marcus started pulling at a leech clinging to his calf. He pulled as hard as he could, but the creepy creature wouldn't release its hold.

"That won't work," Carter said. "There's a better way."

Carter took a box of waterproof matches from his bag. He struck one and handed it off, continuing until everyone had one.

"Watch me," he said and touched his lit match to one of the leeches clinging to his kneecap. As soon as the flame hit, the black blob sizzled and fell off, leaving a small, bloody smear behind.

The others joined the fray, burning off the leeches that were using them as unwilling hosts. Dead leech after dead leech plopped on the ground.

"Burn in hell, you bloodsucking freaks!" Louis was particularly fierce about it.

Once they'd taken care of the visible ones, everyone retreated into the dark to check their more private areas for intruders.

Marcus screamed and shouted the longest string of obscenities Carter had ever heard. But when he rejoined the group, he acted like everything was cool. "Shall we?"

Now leech-free, they continued on, trekking through thick brush and rocky terrain in the dark of the early morning and thick jungle. Carter took the lead, but let his excitement get the better of him. Several times Brad had to call him back to rejoin the others. His lamp provided a minimal amount of light as it was, but when he charged ahead, he left them totally blind.

"Carter, you're too far again," Brad yelled. They'd entered a relatively flat and open area, though their path was littered with rocks, almost like a cobblestone road.

Unable to see where she placed her foot, Yvette smacked her toe on a rock and stumbled forward. If Marcus wasn't there to catch her, she would have bounced her head off another one.

Brad threw his arms up. "Okay, that's it."

Darla and Louis rushed to help Yvette up, only to crash their heads together and nearly fall on top of her.

"We need to wait until the sun comes up," Brad said.

"We can't keep pushing on through the dark. Someone's gonna break their neck."

Carter muttered under his breath, "Whatever, *Dad.*"

Brad tried to get in Carter's face, but he couldn't see where it was. "What did you just say?"

"I didn't say anything," Carter said, smiling, unseen behind the glare of his headlamp.

"Brad's right," Darla said. "It's too dangerous. We can't see a thing. One of us could walk off a cliff or step on a snake or fall in a pit of quicksand." She added before Carter could respond, "And if you call me Mom, I will give you the wedgie to end all wedgies."

"Okay," Carter conceded, "I get it. I've been letting my excitement get the better of me. But I'm your captain. I wouldn't leave you behind or lead you into danger." Then, as an afterthought, he added, "And just for the record, I'm not wearing undies."

"Eww. TMI," Yvette said.

Carter walked away from the huddled group to find a thicket of bushes. He snapped off the largest stick he could find, then ripped a strip of cloth from his shirt and wrapped it around the stick.

"Give me your suntan lotion," he said to Louis.

Louis clutched his bag. "Why would I do that? The sun isn't up. And you have the complexion of an Irish ghost. No amount of tanning lotion is going to bronze you up."

"Just hand it over," Carter demanded. "Don't make your captain ask twice."

Reluctantly, Louis took his prized bottle of Hello Kitty Tanning Oil from his bag and handed it to Carter. "Pineapple-coconut," he said with pouty lips. "My favorite. And it's hella expensive, so please be frugal."

The words had barely left his mouth when Carter popped the top and doused the strip of cloth with the oil. He tossed the bottle back to Louis before striking a match and lighting the cloth.

With a whoosh of heat and light, the torch burst into flame. Everyone jumped back, shielding their eyes from the sudden onslaught of light.

"Necessity is the mother of all invention," Carter grumbled in his pirate voice.

The crew immediately began scouring the area for sticks, and tore cloth from their own shirts to make their torches. Louis gave the tanning oil up for lost and passed the bottle around.

Darla took the matches first. "Okay, but seriously, we need to be careful with this. I don't want to be responsible for burning down the rainforest." She struck her match and lit the torch. "Mother nature is more valuable than any treasure."

When all the torches were lit, the group set off once again. They looked like a parade of fireflies.

17

Meanwhile...

Proud military man and owner of twenty-four-inch biceps that could curl a suitcase of bowling balls, Major North continued his search for the cadet that got away.

Major North knew the survival store well, even though he had lived on the opposite side of the country. He'd been stationed in this region once upon a time. And even if he hadn't been, it was only smart to research potential assets before venturing out. He could have named ten sites to resupply at if the need arose. Surplus stores, army depots, gun shows, a few aficionados with exceptional gun collections. If things went *Red Dawn*, he'd know how to get strapped in a blink.

Regardless, this store required no research. He knew the owner from way back.

"Ten-hut!" North yelled as he walked in.

The man behind the counter, a muscular man with the obvious beginnings of a gut in his lower forties, snapped to attention and saluted crisply.

"Starting to sag around the midsection, soldier," Major North barked.

"Don't see much action these days, sir," the man replied.

North stopped in front of him, their noses almost touching. "That's no excuse for going soft."

The man smiled. "It's good to see you, sir."

Major North took his hand in a strong, bone-crunching shake. "You too, Tolliver. Thanks for the help. I know it's last-minute."

"I owe you my life, sir," Tolliver said. "Whatever you need, it's yours." Tolliver's attention shifted to the door and the three who just entered. "They with you?"

Ms. Roberts sauntered to Major North's side while the cadets marveled at the gear hanging on the walls. She draped herself over his arm. "Certainly am," she said.

North politely slipped out from under her. He gestured to the old, rabbit-eared TV that sat on the counter. A news report of the six missing kids played. "One of them is hers. Another's mine. And I mean to collect them. Just need a ride."

Tolliver nodded. "Roger that. Follow me." He led them toward the back of the store, through a cluttered storage room and into a wide, paved lot behind the building. "That work for ya?"

Major North's companions gazed at the helicopter like it was a dinosaur, or a dragon, or some other mythical beast deserving of awe. But the major looked nervous. The old rotorcraft was rusty and in disrepair. It looked like it hadn't been flown in years. Maybe decades.

"You sure this thing will fly?" the major asked.

Tolliver looked offended. "She's a workhorse, not a beauty queen. But she'll get you where you're going."

Major North breathed in deep, and let it out slow. His eyes danced over the helicopter, full of hesitation. By the time he'd fully exhaled, he'd made up his mind.

"Mount up," he said.

No one moved. His hesitation seemed to have worn off on them.

"Mount up!"

The cadets rushed forward, shouting "Valley Forge Military Academy! Hoo-rah!" and climbed into the helicopter.

Ms. Roberts brushed her hand against Major North as she passed. "This is going to be so much fun."

18

The firefly parade broke through the thick of the jungle, coming out into a boulder-strewn clearing. The huge rocks looked like squat giants, sitting down to dinner. Carter and Darla held the map and iPad next to each other, studying their similarities.

They'd done it. They'd arrived at the "x".

Fire lit in Carter's belly. "Aye, 'tis the place. The game's afoot."

"That's Sherlock Holmes," Darla corrected. "Not pirates."

"Sherlock seemed like a bit of a pirate, himself," Carter said.

"Let's spread out, see if we can find something," Brad said.

The crew fanned out, waving their torches to investigate the clearing.

"There's lots of *something*," Yvette said. "Rocks, trees, dirt. Be more specific."

"I don't know," Brad said with a shrug. "Something, you know, treasure-y."

"Big help," Yvette grumbled.

Just under his bubbling excitement, Carter felt something else—a tingling on the back of his neck, like someone stood behind him, breathing on him. His gut pinched. A rustling on the south side of the clearing drew his attention. He spun, waving his torch in an orange arc.

He crept toward it, knowing deep down that it was a terrible idea. Images flashed in his head—a hungry panther, man-eating anaconda, zombie pirates. But he kept walking closer to the sound. Only a few feet from the edge of the clearing.

Then a rustling on the north side. He spun back. But now his back was exposed. He spun again. The zombie pirates had him surrounded.

He stopped, took a deep breath. "It's nothing," he told himself. "Just the jungle. Lots of life, lots of noise. But nothing to be concerned about." He rejoined the search.

Carter walked around one of the larger boulders, running his hand along the craggy side. He let himself feel each bump and crack. Then a soft patch of moss. And then...

Wait.

Carter felt something in the moss. Or, really, a *lack* of something. There was a depression, and not a natural one. It was too precise. He traced the pattern with his finger, and bells went off in his head.

"I found something!" he yelled to the others.

They all came running. Even Brad looked eager to see what Carter had found. In the torchlight, he looked exactly how Carter remembered him when he was little.

"Feast your eyes," Carter said.

They all groaned.

"Moss," Marcus said, sounding annoyed. "Feast your eyes on this," he said, holding up a stick. "And look over there. I see some dirt."

Carter couldn't help the self-satisfied smile as he traced the impression on the rock with his finger for all to see.

"Yeah. Moss," Yvette said.

Carter held up the four-lock box he'd taken from the museum. He pointed to a pattern on the side of it, and then traced the impression again.

"Identical," he said triumphantly.

"I think you're seeing what you want to see," Louis said with folded arms and an unimpressed tone.

Carter growled. "Seriously?" He scraped the moss away to reveal a carving that matched the box plain as day.

They couldn't deny it now. One by one, each crew member's face lit with astonishment.

"Oh, yeah," Marcus said, unable to hide his excitement. "We're getting into some Indiana Jones stuff now."

"Spread out and look for more," Carter said.

The crew broke apart and swarmed the boulder like flies on poop. Marcus discovered another marking on the opposite side. Brad and Darla found one on the left. Louis and Yvette found one on the right.

Carter compared the symbols on the box to each carving discovered on the boulder. All matched. "Well," he said, slapping the rock. "You're in the middle of nowhere and you need to hide some treasure. What better place to do it than under a super huge rock?"

Marcus pushed against the rock. "This thing weighs a ton. No way we're moving it."

The crew stood staring at the rock, not quite defeated, but not nearly as excited as they were moments ago.

"The pyramids!" Darla shouted. "The Egyptians used levers and fulcrums to move huge rocks to build the pyramids. We can do the same to move this boulder."

Marcus snorted. "Everyone knows *aliens* built the pyramids. Don't you watch the History Channel?"

Louis dismissed Marcus. "Work smarter, not harder. I like where your head's at, girl." Louis gestured for the crew to follow him into the forest. "Let's find our lever."

Brad and Marcus found a fallen palm tree. Yvette and Louis rolled one of the smaller rocks. They placed the rock half the length of the tree, which was a few yards away from the rock. Then they placed the tree over it, jabbing the far end under the boulder.

Darla surveyed the creation, seeming satisfied. "Looks good." She grabbed onto the end of the tree and hung. Nothing. She swung her legs up and over so that she lay atop the log. Nothing.

"Come on," she said to the crew. "I'm not heavy enough. We need everyone up here if we want this thing to move."

One by one, the crew climbed onto the log. Each person added to the complexity of their balancing act. One grabbed onto the next to steady themselves. If one fell, they all went down.

Still, the boulder did not move.

"Okay," Darla groaned, tensing every muscle to keep her balance. "Maybe if we do a little hop?"

"Loco," Yvette said.

"Agreed," Louis said. "Girl done lost her mind."

"It'll be fine." Darla pumped her legs, and the others followed suit. "One, two…"

Snap!

The tree cracked in half, and the mass of teenage pirates crashed to the ground like an oversized human pretzel, elbows and knees and heads smacking together. They rolled apart, all trying to find the wind that had just been knocked out of them.

"Well that didn't work as planned," Darla groaned.

"You think?" Marcus coughed.

"We need a thicker log," Darla said.

The crew went back to scouring the forest. They soon came back with another palm, this one much sturdier than the last. They set it up the same as the last one.

"Okay," Louis said. "But we're still not heavy enough. We already know that."

"I have an idea," Brad said.

The crew looked on anxiously as Brad climbed on top of the boulder. Excitement fluttered in Carter's belly. His brother and first mate was about to do something truly brash and reckless. He loved it!

"This looks like probably the worst idea ever," Louis said.

Once on top, Brad stepped to the edge of the boulder. He bent his knees, pumped his legs. "No, this is definitely the *best* idea. We don't need a lot of steady force to lift the boulder; we need one quick jolt. Like smashing a bottle. You slam it on the ground, not try to squeeze it until it cracks. It's science."

"Spoken like a true scientist," Louis said, his voice dripping with sarcasm.

The crew stepped back.

Carter counted down. On one, Brad jumped off the boulder. His body became a rocket, aimed straight down at the end of their lever. He hit it, pushed through his legs with all his strength. The tree bent. And then it snapped back and launched him high into the air, like he had bounded off a trampoline. He soared like a tennis ball in a long arc and crashed into the bushes at the edge of the clearing.

All were silent, holding their breath, hoping their first mate wasn't seriously injured. Or worse.

"Brad? Are you okay?" Darla asked.

"Yeah," Brad groaned. "Science has failed me."

The collective laughter the crew had been struggling to hold back burst out. Carter cocked his head, thinking he heard some more rustling at the edges of the clearing, or some kind of chirping, maybe. He looked, but saw nothing.

Once Brad had climbed out of his bush of embarrassment, he called the crew around. "I did some thinking."

"While you were in your bush?" Marcus said through a chuckle.

Brad shot him a vicious stare. "As a matter of fact, yes. It's the only quiet place I've found since stepping on that boat. Anyway, I did some thinking, and I think I gave up on science too quickly. I still think my plan could work."

"Don't say it," Louis said, his eyes closed.

"We just need more force."

"Aye," Yvette said, throwing her arms up. "*El es loco tambien!*"

Despite their protests, Brad, Marcus and Carter gathered atop the boulder just moments later. They inched toward the edge of the boulder as one huddled mass.

"I don't know who's crazier," Yvette said from the

ground. "Brad for doing this again, or you fools for following him."

"It'll work," Brad said. "Trust me. It's science."

"I don't think you know what science is," Yvette said.

Carter counted down again. They jumped. The log bent. And they soared through the air like human missiles, crashing in the same bushes of embarrassment that caught Brad minutes earlier.

"Guys are dumb," Darla said. "No offense," she added to Louis.

"None taken," Louis said. "I don't know what it is about external plumbing that makes boys so stupid."

The guys emerged from the bushes, bruised and with little cuts and scratches all over their faces.

"Science let me down again," Brad said, rubbing a quickly forming bruise on his forehead.

"Don't blame science," Darla said. "According to Louis, you should blame your—"

"Avast!" Carter stood firm, planting his feet like they were cemented to the ground. He grabbed his unlit torch and swung it in a wide arc, then pointed it like a sword at the edge of the clearing. "Cleave them to the brisket!"

The crew followed the point of his torch-sword.

The two pirates who'd attacked them at sea walked out of the jungle.

19

Elbow-deep in the sputtering engine of *Salty Walty*, the crazed fisherman's final voyage may have come to an early end.

Walter hadn't taken his boat to sea in years. He knew the stories about him. He knew the legends. And he didn't care. He knew his reasons, for what they were worth.

But their worth was nothing compared to the value of that girl, lost out there.

Either way, he never thought he'd be out at sea again. The salty wind felt good on his face. The rocking of the boat was like his mother lulling him to sleep in his crib—if his crib was a broken-down heap, that is.

To say he hadn't kept up with maintaining old *Salty* was a major understatement. He may have let her slide downhill a bit over the years, but hadn't they both? He hadn't looked at her engine since parking her in his driveway. He was foolish to think it would look the same as it had that day.

Not that he would know the difference. The old fool was half blind. That's why he'd really taken her off the water. He couldn't see well enough to sail her and was too stubborn to do anything about it. Couldn't admit to himself that he was going downhill.

And what did that get him? A house full of junk, trinkets to trick him into thinking he was still a fisherman, a man of the sea. Stubborn old man lost the only thing he ever cared about because he wouldn't go to see an eye doctor.

He'd let himself and *Salty* fall apart.

A fresh cloud of acrid black smoke puffed into his face. It reeked of burnt motor oil. He rubbed the stinging from his eyes and tried to see through the haze, into the small compartment lit only by his old kerosene lantern. Any way he saw it, the engine was done for. It was amazing that she got him out this far, to the edge of the Bahamas island chain.

Walter fell back onto his butt and buried his face in his hands. Motor oil smeared across his cheeks like war paint. The engine gave one last sputter, and died.

Now, *Salty Walty* drifted aimlessly, an old broken-down thing.

"Lotta good times," he said, running his hand along the deck. "Good times. The storm of '86. Hurricane in '93. That run-in with pirates off the coast of Haiti. Put those fools in the drink just as quick as I seen the crossbones around their necks. Brutes was what they were. Didn't care nothin' for the code." He rested his head against the rail and looked up at the stars. "Seen some action, you and me. Reckon that's all for us, though."

And then, like the changing of the tides, the sinking sense of the end washed away. The sea air blew the doom right out of his head, leaving memories of adventure, and in that moment he knew he wasn't done.

Not yet, anyway.

"Screw this," he said. He stood and whipped off his clothes, revealing a full-body bathing suit beneath, complete with arm straps and stripes, like one from an old movie. He slung his collapsible fishing rod like a sword over his shoulder. He stood on the rail and took one last look at *Salty*.

He bowed his head and recited a prayer for the old girl. "Disturb us, Lord, to dare more boldly, to venture on wilder seas where storms will show Your mastery, where losing sight of land, we shall find the stars."

And then he dove overboard.

20

Carter prepared to run the brigands through. "Relax, kid," Nestor said, his arms up as though surrendering. "We don't mean you any harm."

"Hornswaggle," Carter said. "You tried to kill us. And you'll refer to me as Captain."

"Whoa, no way," JJ said. "We just wanted to steal your boat. *You* tried to kill *us*."

"We were defending ourselves," Carter said.

"You left us stranded in the middle of nowhere on a sinking ship," JJ argued.

"Better than you deserved." Carter pointed the tip of his torch toward JJ's legs. "I should set you pants on fire for being such a liar."

Nestor stepped between JJ and Carter, his arms still up. "Look, I ain't gonna lie. We would'a done the same to you if we had the chance. And, truth is, we've been through a lot to get here just so we could repay you for sinking us, and making us look like fools. But, now that we're here, I gotta say, I'm impressed."

Carter felt a crack run through his guard. His cheeks blushed a little. "Say what now?"

"You're the captain of this crew, right? Like you said,"

Nestor said. "It's plain to see. You fought us off with nothing but *MacGyver*'d scuba tanks. Sunk us. Made your way all the way out here. And now it looks like you're really on to something with that map. I thought you were just some punk kid playing at it before, but it looks like you're the real deal. You're a pirate, kid."

Carter's feet slid from their firm footing. Some actual, wanted-by-the-authorities pirates thought he was the real deal. This was it—the beginning of his pirate reputation. The only thing that was more important to a pirate than his ship: his legend.

"Yeah," Carter said, his chin high. "I am." He lowered his torch.

Brad stepped forward, yanking the torch from Carter's hand and putting it back on the pirates. "Now that we've got the pleasantries out of the way, how about you tell us what you're doing here if not to exact bloody revenge?"

"You the mom of the crew?" Nestor said with a cocky smile.

"First mate," Brad growled. "And the big brother," he added with some ferocity. "Now answer the question."

"We want to see what's under that rock," Nestor said.

"Then you'll need to join my crew and swear loyalty to me," Carter declared.

Before the pirates could answer, Brad yelled, "Whoa! Hold up, I think I need to have a conversation with my captain." He tossed the torch to Yvette. "You and Marcus keep an eye on them."

Marcus pulled out his bat, and he and Yvette took up defensive positions.

Give me a reason, Marcus thought, his hands tightening their grip on his trusty lumber.

Brad grabbed Carter by the arm and pulled him behind the boulder.

"Are you bat-crap crazy?" Brad barked in a poorly hushed voice. "These guys tried to kill us. Now they just pop out of the bushes, and you say *yeah, sure, come along*?"

"We can't move this rock on our own," Carter said, patting it. "And if we can't move it, then we came all this way for nothing."

"Better to waste our time than get killed by pirates."

"*We're* pirates."

"Not like them. Not—"

"Real ones?" Carter finished Brad's thought with a stab of truth. "You still think this is a game?"

Brad jabbed his finger into Carter's chest. "No, I think *you* still think this is a game. I can tell you for sure that those creeps don't think it is. And I told you I would pull the plug if this got out of hand."

"I'm not stupid," Carter said, his anger rising. "I know we can't trust them. But we can't do this without them, either. Besides, you know what they say—keep your friends close, and your enemies closer."

Brad hung his head. "Yvette's right, I am crazy." He peeked around the side of the boulder. Yvette and Marcus still held the pirates at bay. The pirates smiled innocently with mouths full of crooked teeth. "Fine. But Marcus, Yvette, and I will stay on guard. We aren't letting those guys out of our sight. And no one is left alone with them."

"Cool beans," Carter said.

They rejoined the group.

"Let's do this," Carter said. "Time to earn your keep, old guys."

The crew climbed back onto the log, clinging to each other for balance. Once they'd found their footing, the pirates grabbed onto the end of the log and pulled down.

The boulder started to move. It rocked up and teetered on the point of rolling, not sure whether it wanted to commit.

Nestor shoved JJ toward to rock with this foot. "Push."

JJ hunched down like a football player and charged. He drove his shoulder into it, then his hands. He spun around, trying to find the best grip.

Slowly, the boulder tipped. With one final surge, it rolled from its roost, and kept rolling until it crashed into a tree at the edge of the clearing. The lever tree fell to the ground, and the crew crashed on top of Nestor.

They were a mass of cheers and high-fives and fist bumps. For a moment, they almost forgot they were laying on top of a bloodthirsty pirate.

Everyone scrambled to their feet, anxious to see what was uncovered. They shined their torches, swept aside some brush, dug in the sand for any sign of a clue. They continued to do so even after finding nothing.

Louis finally fell onto his back, defeated. "What a rip-off."

Marcus whipped his bat off his back and swung it into a tree.

Darla stared at the impression where the boulder sat. "I don't get it. Why make those carvings if not as a reminder? A way to identify that rock? Why would you need to identify it if there's nothing under it?"

Marcus fell next to Louis. "Because this whole thing is a bunch of crap. Crappity crap crap. CRAP!"

Carter wandered away from the crew, curious, his torch lit. Pirates didn't do anything without a reason. They were savvy, clever, and strategic. They wouldn't waste the time with the box, the map, and the carvings just to mess with some kids hundreds of years later.

He ran his had along the underside of the rock, now facing outward toward the clearing. Suddenly, he felt some indentations. And then he realized they were deliberate, carved. And that they spelled something.

He read them aloud by torchlight. "'Fifty paces to the west, ye shall find my treasure chest. But be forewarned, the path is cruel. You'll live like kings, or die like fools.'"

"Nice poem," Yvette said. "But now isn't the time for limericks or whatever."

"Agreed," said the captain. "But I didn't write it. Whoever carved it into the bottom of this rock did."

The split-second pause that followed felt heavy. The crew was on the edge of being broken, and they took that moment to question whether they believed Carter, whether they even cared, whether they wanted to press on. But it only took that second for them to decide. They all sprung to their feet and ran to investigate. They read it again, out loud, to themselves. And cared, they did.

"Treasure chest?"

"Live like kings?"

"It's real! It's really real!"

"Die like fools?" Brad was always such a downer.

"Which way is west?"

Everyone pointed in opposite directions. But a true captain always knows which way is north, so he always knows which was is west. He returned to the boulder's original nesting place, and began counting off.

"One, two, three..."

21

High above the Caribbean, the determined ex-army man soared closer to his target.

Major North had forgotten how much he missed this—flying through the dead of night, geared up for a drop behind enemy lines. The mission. The team. Well, maybe not *this* team. A couple cadets and a bizarrely forward and clingy orphanage director. But the rest of it, the feeling, the rush before reaching the LZ. The unknown lurking out there in the dark jungle, just beyond the reach of the helicopter's spotlight…

It was time for him to leave the military. He knew that. But not because he wanted to. Politics. The whole thing had become too political. He'd enlisted for adventure. That was what he'd wanted when he signed up, fresh out of high school. And that was certainly what he got, for a while anyway. But someone once told him that if you do what you love and you're good at it, then you'll get promoted, and promoted, and promoted, and soon you'd be further away from the thing you loved than you were before you'd started.

He didn't believe it, of course. Sounded absurd. But after a few decades in the service, it dawned on him just how true it was.

So he retired.

And started working at a school.

He couldn't remember for the life of him what had driven him to that decision. He'd never been overly fond of children. Maybe it was still that fresh sense of adventure that came off youth like the black diesel perfume of a chopper. Maybe he hoped it would rub off on him.

It hadn't.

If anything, it had just made him bitter, training them to set off on their own adventures while his seemed to be long behind him.

Until today, he'd been certain he'd never run another mission. He hated losing a cadet, but, in a way, he was happy the Humbolt kid had bolted.

Now he had something to chase.

"We're coming up on Eleuthera," Tolliver said through the headset.

Major North leaned out the door to get a better look as they hovered over the island. "There," he said, pointing down to a clearing. "Set us down there."

Moments later, the helicopter touched down. The old bird creaked and crunched. It probably thought its adventuring days were behind it as well.

The cadets jumped out first. For once, Major North found their youthful exuberance tolerable. A little contagious, even.

The major locked it down. Couldn't let emotion cloud judgment. That was how you lost men. Or, how you lost cadets and an orphanage director.

Major North exited the helicopter and walked around to an exterior cargo hatch. He popped it open, and struggled to contain a gasp of excitement.

Lock it down!

There, looking back at him were some truly impressive pieces of military hardware. The most modern weaponry and tactical gear. They could storm a bunker with this stuff. They had a—

Ms. Roberts pushed past the cadets and reached into the hatch. She took out a long, cylindrical weapon with levers and buttons all over it.

Major North tensed. He thought maybe she was just eccentric. A little unhinged at the most. But maybe she really was crazy.

"Don't move," he said quietly, taking a very slow and cautioned step toward her. "That's—"

She hit the lever and flipped open the weapon's six-shot revolver-like cylinder. "A Milkor MGL forty-millimeter grenade launcher," she said, finishing the major's sentence. "American made. Six shots. Fires everything from HE rounds to less lethal bean bag projectiles, designed to put down a tango without any permanent damage." She speed-loaded the weapon with specialized bean bag rounds and snapped the cylinder shut. "Perfect for apprehension and interrogation."

Major North's jaw sat on the jungle floor. He suddenly felt very sorry for Humbolt. "Where'd you learn that?"

"101st Airborne."

If his jaw could have fallen any further, it would have." You're a Screamin' Eagle?"

"Heck no," she answered. "But I dated one for a stitch." She pumped her eyebrows, but the major could see that her eyes didn't shimmer with that same sparkle of mischief. "Gave me some weapons training, y'know what I mean?" His smile fell at the corners. "And a daughter."

There was some sadness in her voice, but she did her best to hide it. And she did it quickly. "Well? Let's do this thing." Her face lit up in a way that Major North now realized was familiar.

He'd seen it on countless cadets. Kids like Humbolt with a chip on their shoulder, but damned if you'd know it, because they put on a face for the world. A strong, happy face, so no one was the wiser as to what was really going on inside.

Major North loaded his Milkor. "Yeah, we're doing this."

The cadets reached for the open cargo hatch. "What do we get?"

Major North slapped their hands away. "No guns for minors." He removed two rods with forked tongs at the ends. "You get this. More than enough to take down your enemy."

The initial look of despair quickly left their faces after each cadet sparked their cattle prod. Little sparks of blue danced in their eyes. They said in unison, "Valley Forge Military Academy! Hoo-rah!"

The company set off from the chopper toward the shore. They all hunched down on the beach, staring at the sailboat anchored thirty yards out at sea. All of the lights were off. It rocked like a piece of driftwood as the tide rolled in.

"What's the plan, sir?" the cadets said.

Major North studied the situation. He pinpointed the goal, listed his assets and the challenges ahead. He smiled at the cadets. "You two have your swimming certifications, right? Two of the best swimmers in the academy, if I recall."

The cadets gulped, and nodded.

"You two are going to do some recon."

The cadets stripped off their gear and dropped it in a pile on the beach. They waded into the water, moving slowly and quietly. Then they were gone, swimming through the dark.

Ms. Roberts sighed contentedly and laid back on her elbows. "Isn't this romantic?"

The major tensed. He felt like an enemy had snuck up behind him and put a machete to his neck.

"The beach," Ms. Roberts continued. "The sound of the water. The gentle breeze just ever so casually tousling my hair in the flirtiest of ways. The full moon. Just the two of us."

"It won't be just the two of us for long," Major North said.

"But it's just the two of us *right now*," Ms. Roberts said, patting the sand next to her, inviting Major North to sit. "So relax. Take a load off."

"We're on mission," the major said. "There is no relaxing."

"You don't like to live in the moment, do you?" A serious edge had crept into her voice, but still wore mischief like a blanket.

"No," the major answered. "One can't strategize while living in the moment."

Ms. Roberts folded her hands behind her head and laid back on the sand. "This moment is the only one that matters. Until the next moment. Looking ahead, looking back, I think that'll just disappoint you."

Major North thought on this while he looked out

at the water. It was a heavier thought than he ever expected to hear from her. And one he, thankfully, did not need to respond to, courtesy of the return of the cadets.

They rose from the water, panting, graceless. Tim flopped onto the beach like a fish sucking for air. Kevin doubled over, gasping.

"Report," Major North ordered.

"I think," Tim said in syllables broken by breathlessness.

"They're sleeping," Kevin finished.

"Perfect," Major North said. He slipped his grenade launcher off his shoulder, and began stacking all their gear in some nearby brush. The others did the same. Then he took a waterproof bag and filled it with a few things he would need. He zipped it closed, and smiled. "Let's go swimming."

The cadets groaned but followed Major North into the water. The major looked over his shoulder, half expecting Ms. Roberts to be right by his side. But she wasn't. He felt a pinch of guilt in his gut for every time he wished she would disappear. She could be abrasive, true. But she was upfront, and he respected that. There was a genuine quality to her that could be endearing.

When she wasn't being a chore.

He checked his gear one last time. You could never be too prepared. When he turned back toward the sea, he saw Ms. Roberts already in a full front crawl heading toward the boat.

He smiled and dove forward.

They reached the sailboat in just a few minutes. Major North climbed the side first. Once on the deck, he reached down and pulled both cadets up at once.

He reached back again for Ms. Roberts, but she was already climbing.

He was so used to teaching, to showing how to do things, to providing assistance. She didn't need any of that.

The four of them skulked across the deck and paused at the hatch that led below. Major North unzipped the bag and pulled out a cylinder about eight inches long with a pin in one end and lever on the side. Flash-bang grenade. Talk about a wake-up call.

Using his fingers, the major counted down from three. Then he pulled the pin, released the lever, and dropped the grenade down the hatch. The four of them hunched down, covering their eyes and ears.

A concussive wave of sound smacked the underside of the deck, punching Major North in the gut, knocking the wind out of him. Not allowing it to slow him down, the major launched to his feet. He ran down the stairs, ready to catch the kids off-guard.

Ms. Roberts and the cadet ran down behind him.

"Waste of a good grenade," Ms. Roberts said as she looked around at the empty boat.

The cadets cringed.

"Sleeping?" the major said.

"Well, it was dark and super quiet," Kevin said.

"So, maybe we assumed?" Tim said.

Major North turned on them. "Assume again, and you'll be walking home." He marched topside.

Kevin looked confused. "But, we're on an island. How can we…?"

Tim smacked his brother in the back of the head. "That's the point."

Ms. Roberts pushed past them and followed the major.

"Forty-eight, forty-nine, fifty!"

Without direction or order, the crew dove for the ground like a pack of rabid moles. They dug into the earth, flinging dirt everywhere, turning the grassy area where they'd stopped into a minefield of holes.

As the sun peaked over the horizon, the pale light of morning shone on Eleuthera. It illuminated the ground around Carter, and the cliff's edge only yards from the crew. His stomach turned when he thought about trudging through the dark, unaware of the sudden rocky plummet. If that engraving said sixty paces, he might have paced right over the edge.

A roar of grumbling from the dig site drew him away from the cliff.

"I give up," Nestor said, his hands and face completely covered in dirt. "There's nothing here."

"There has to be," Carter argued. "You saw the rock."

"Hate to break it to you, kid, but pirates ain't always the most trustworthy of people. Maybe it's a misdirect." Nestor climbed out of his hole. He kicked JJ, who had fallen asleep sometime during the excavation. "Get up. We need to talk."

JJ stirred and wiped dirt and sleep from his eyes. The two walked off and out of sight.

Brad dropped down next to Darla, who had also fallen asleep. He looked as dejected as Nestor.

Darla woke slowly, sitting up and resting her head on Brad's shoulder. "We rich?"

"No, just dirty."

She looked around, taking stock of the situation. "Where'd our pirate friends run off to?"

"In congress in the bushes," Carter said, gesturing with his chin to the spot in the jungle they'd disappeared to.

"I thought someone was supposed to keep an eye on them." She leaned around to look in Brad's face.

He stared off at nothing in particular with an intense, thoughtful look in his eyes.

She waved her hand in front of his face. "Anyone home?"

Suddenly, Brad leapt to his feet. He ran off down the same path they'd taken from the boulder.

"What'd you do to him?" Carter asked Darla.

She shrugged.

"Tummy troubles?" Carter suggested. "He is, after all, a nervous pooper."

"Gross," Darla answered.

A few moments later, Brad emerged from the jungle, taking long, deliberate strides, and counting as he went.

"I did that already," Carter said. "I know how to count."

Brad kept going. As he reached the spot where they'd been digging, he said, "Thirty-five, thirty-six."

He shot Carter a knowing look as he continued on. "Forty-eight, forty-nine..."

Brad stopped at the cliff's edge and pointed over. "Fifty."

The crew gathered along the cliff's edge, looking over.

"There probably weren't too many eleven-year-old pirates," Brad said. "I'm guessing whoever wrote that riddle was a little bit older and had longer legs. They meant fifty man paces, not fifty little kid paces."

Carter nodded, shrugging off the attempt at insult. "Okay, then why don't you go ahead and take that fiftieth step?" Maybe he didn't shrug it off completely.

Backing away from the ledge, Louis tugged on Yvette's sleeve. "I need to, uh, powder my nose. Will you watch?"

"Gross."

"Not me! Keep watch," Louis said, the urgency of his situation straining his voice. "I don't want a snake or something crawling up on me while I'm copping a squat."

Reluctantly, Yvette agreed. It was mandated by the unspoken girl code.

The two disappeared into the jungle as the others scratched their chins about the riddle.

"Maybe the treasure is all the way down there," Marcus said. "Do we climb down?"

"Maybe the riddle was just what we thought it was," Brad said. "A misdirect. A way to get people searching for the treasure to *die like fools*."

Walking off a cliff is a bad way to go. Certainly a foolish one.

Carter turned away from the cliff, hoping to clear his head and get a fresh perspective on the whole thing.

But that isn't at all what he saw. Instead, he watched as Louis and Yvette were ushered out of the jungle at gunpoint.

"Battle stations!"

Carter's order snapped the crew from their contemplation.

The two military academy cadets sprinted around the major and ran straight for them. Marcus sprung forward, quick-drawing his bat.

"Chill. I got this," he said.

The cadets skidded to a halt just out of face-smashing range. "Valley Forge Military Academy! Hoo-rah!" They each pressed a button on the prods they carried, and the ends sparked and crackled with electricity.

Brad stepped forward, shoulder-to-shoulder with Marcus. "Take another step and this ends badly."

"Yeah," Tim said. "For you."

Major North stepped up behind the cadets. They flanked him like a pair of guard dogs. "This has gone far enough."

Darla, incensed, screamed from behind Brad. "Who the hell are you to tell us anything? You're totally bat-crap, man. Why would you follow us all the way out here?"

"Hello, honey," came a voice from behind the major. "Miss me?" Ms. Roberts stepped out from behind the musclebound goon.

Color drained from Darla's face. "What in the actual crap is happening right now?"

"Playtime's over," Ms. Roberts said. "You're all coming with us."

"Why should we?" Brad asked.

Major North chuckled, as if it were a crazy question.

"Because those who have the weapons make the rules." The major turned suddenly, the muzzle of his grenade launcher following and landing on Nestor and JJ who'd just wandered back from wherever they'd snuck off to. "You two, over there with the rest. Keep your hands where I can see 'em."

"We aren't with them," JJ said.

"You are now," answered the major.

Carter pushed past Marcus and Brad, his chin high and chest out. "If anyone's to be punished, 'tis I, Captain Lackbeard. My crew won't take the lashings meant for my back."

"You're a stand-up kid," the major said. "You take your responsibilities seriously. Take care of your crew. I respect that. You're also in serious need of a psych eval, but that's beyond the point." He aimed his grenade launcher at Carter. "Are you truly ready to accept the burden of leadership?"

Carter shut his eyes tight, but still held his chin high. "Aye."

A metal click sounded. Removing the safety probably. Several clicks. What could that be?

Carter opened his eyes to see a fishing line being cast from somewhere in the jungle. As soon as it wrapped around the major's gun, it yanked backwards. The gun popped out of the major's hands and landed with a thud on the ground.

Before anyone could react, the line was cast again. This time, it wrapped around Ms. Roberts's gun and yanked it from her hands.

All were dumbfounded except Walter, who strutted out of the jungle like a peacock, shining his knuckles on his chest. "I still got it."

"You crazy old geezer," Ms. Roberts yelled. "What are you doing here?"

"Saving these kids."

"From what?" Ms. Roberts was about to march over and deck the old man.

"From us," Nestor said. "Well, he tried, anyway."

All eyes shifted to the pirates. They cradled the grenade launchers in their arms like cute little babies capable of wanton destruction.

"Exactly," Walter said. "Now, who are you guys, exactly?"

Nestor ignored him. He ignored everyone except Carter. "You and me got unfinished business."

"I thought we'd put that behind us," Carter said.

"You thought wrong."

The next few seconds were a blur of shock and awe and pain. Carter remembered the sound like fireworks shooting off, before they exploded in the sky—that hollow *pop*. Then Brad appeared in front of him. He was floating, suspended in midair. Until the beanbag fired from the pirate's gun hit him in the chest. The wicked force of it knocked Brad backwards.

He collided with Carter.

Carter fell back. He planted his foot to catch himself. At least, he would have...if there'd been any ground behind him to stand on.

His back foot went over the edge of the cliff, and the rest of his body followed.

23

Carter's mother—Eileen was her name—he'd seen her only in a few pictures, the ones Brad kept sewn into the lining of his jacket. Brad looked like her. Carter might have, too, but it's hard to look at yourself and realize who you look like. People had commented that Carter looked like Brad, so maybe he did look like her.

He liked to think that he was like her. That his pirate soul had come from her. He didn't remember her beyond some hazy recollections, some echoes of her presence at the museum that one time. But he thought he had a sense of her.

She was a wild girl when she was a child. Other girls didn't want to play with her because she played boys' games. Boys didn't want to play with her because she played boys' games better than they did. So she played alone. But that didn't bother her. Because she had an infinite number of worlds to play in. She created a new one every day, filled with people and creatures that were happy to see her. Unless they were villains, of course, and then they ran at the sight of her.

But she wasn't the hero of these worlds. She didn't give

herself a cape and save the day. She would, obviously, if the opportunity presented itself, but that wasn't her purpose. Adventure was her purpose. Adventure that brought her outside of the rules. Outside of the role little girls were meant to play. And that scared people.

When people are scared of you, they push you away.

So, maybe she was lonely sometimes, but she wasn't sad.

Because she had a pirate's soul.

Carter saw her has he fell. She looked like she did in her pictures, but she was…more. He couldn't explain it. It seemed like his memory of her had stepped out of his head and wrapped itself around the shell of a real person. Like she became real. Flesh and blood.

She leaned over, put her face so close to his, close enough that he could see the waves in her eyes. "Never give up. Never surrender. Never stop being who you are." Her words took hold of him. Her hair wrapped around him.

And then she was gone.

For half a second, Carter felt like he was weightless. But as he woke up and realized where he was, his heart kicked into overdrive. Every muscle fiber in his body tightened, and he felt like the heaviest thing in the world.

He was tangled in a nest of vines that snaked out from the edge of the cliff. They wrapped around his waist and legs, dangling him upside down. He stared straight down at the rocky, churning sea, and it stared back at him.

He tried to study it, to find out exactly which vine was holding him up, to find a way to climb out, but he was too scared to move.

He heard yelling from above. Screams, angry shouting.

They didn't know he was there. They thought he was gone.

He needed to let them know he was still alive. At least, he was for the moment. "Help!" he yelled as loud as he thought he could without shaking loose from the tangle. But it wasn't loud enough. His plea just dropped into the foam down below.

He took a deep breath, held it, and then let out a quick burst of noise. Then he waited.

The yelling up above stopped.

And then, "Did you hear that?" It sounded like Louis.

Carter took another deep breath, and let out another quick burst of sound.

"Carter, is that you?" Brad's voice fell from the top of the cliff. A chorus of thankful cheers sounded from the sky. "Are you okay?"

"Yeah," Carter yelled back. "Peachy."

A vine snapped. Carter's gut lurched as he fell. But he only fell inches before the rigging of vines caught him again and swung him toward the cliff face.

And then they all snapped.

Carter braced for the worst. But, really, how can you brace for a long fall and a sudden, splattery stop? Luckily, his fall wasn't that far. He slammed onto rocky ground, knocking the wind of his lungs.

"Carter!" Brad yelled.

"I'm all right!" Carter yelled back through gasps. "You were right about that fiftieth pace!" He was standing inside a dark cave that cut back into the cliff.

He could see a few yards into the cave, only what was illuminated by the light of the rising sun. And as amazingly brave and daring as Captain Lackbeard was, he didn't want to run into a deep, dark cave all by himself.

"We're coming down," Brad yelled.

A chorus of voices followed, but Carter couldn't be bothered to listen. They were doing their own thing now, and all he could do was wait.

Wait and explore what little of the cave he could see. He studied the ground, looking for signs of inevitable booby traps. If anything, he knew that much for sure. Pirates loved booby traps.

But he found nothing special. So he stepped a bit further into the cave, just beyond the veil of darkness. He ran his hand along the wall. Something jutted out the rock, something manmade. He leaned in for a closer look, and could barely make out the edges. But what he couldn't see, he could smell.

Oil.

He fished the waterproof matches out of his pocket. Two left. He took a deep breath, and struck. The firelight showed a lantern mounted to the wall. He touched the match to the reservoir of oil, and it sparked to life.

Out of the corner of Carter's eye, he watched as a spark ran from the lit lantern down a cannon fuse strung along the cave wall. As it traveled, new lanterns were lit at odd intervals. Soon, a trail of light extended deep into the cave and disappeared around a corner fifty yards in.

He didn't know whether he would have gone on alone at that point, now that he could see. He wrestled with the decision for just a minute before the rappel rope fell over the edge of the cliff and dangled in front of the cave.

Cadet Tim slid down a second later. "I'm here to rescue you, civilian." Tim swung his legs until he was moving like a pendulum, back and forth. When he was close enough, Carter grabbed the rope and pulled Tim in.

Then came Louis, Marcus, Walter, and the second cadet, Kevin. Carter froze when the pirates came down next. "Hold up, correct me if I'm wrong, but didn't they just double-cross us and knock me off a cliff?"

Brad filled Carter in on what happened in the moments when he dangled over certain doom.

Apparently, Nestor was all full of regret. Never tossed a kid over a cliff in all his dubious adventures, Carter guessed. Anyway, he handed his gun over to Major North even though he could have simply bean-bagged them all and run off.

"That's right," Nestor said, his voice meek, but serious. "I'm turning over a new leaf."

Major North appeared in the cave opening. "I'll believe it when I see it." He rocked back, and then swung forward and jumped into the cave on his own. No help required. "Until then, we'll keep an eye on them. Isn't that right cadets?"

"Hoo-rah!"

"And I'll be taking charge of this operation."

"You keep thinking that, Captain Bench Press." Carter stepped around the major like he wasn't even there. "As soon as the rest of my crew gets here, we're off. You can do whatever you want."

Carter joined Brad at the mouth of the cave. Before Carter could speak, Brad wrapped him up in the tightest bear hug of his life. Brad made a series of noises, half-words, the beginnings of a heartfelt sentiment that tripped over itself and fell on its face.

135

So Carter squeezed him back, letting him know that no words were necessary.

As they broke apart, a shouting match from above grew so intense, Carter thought it might cause a cave in.

"Why did you come along, anyway?" Darla had razors in her voice. "Just so you could torment me some more?"

"I'm trying to keep you from making the same mistakes I did." Ms. Roberts cut back

"You're trying to control my life."

"I just want what's best for you. And you can't see that right now because you're a mess of teenage hormones."

"Seems like you're trying to keep me locked in the house with you."

"Exactly the opposite," Ms. Roberts said. "I want you to be free. I want you to go on all the adventures you could ever hope to go on. And you won't be able to do that if you tie yourself to Brad Humbolt."

Darla yelled down to the cave. "Get ready for me. I'm coming down."

The rappel line jostled as it took her weight, tensed nearly as much as Brad's jaw. He and Ms. Roberts rarely openly clashed. Brad rarely openly clashed with anyone besides Carter. But that didn't mean they liked each other. Seeing the torment she inflicted on Darla was enough to secure her place in Brad's bad graces.

It was just one of many reasons Carter hated her. She'd made his life miserable for as long as he could remember. The second he stepped out of line, even slid his pinky toe over the line, she cracked like a whip. He was used to adults not caring about him. The foster parents he'd had tended toward dismissive. He wouldn't say neglectful—it wasn't like they starved him. But none of them particularly cared. He was there, that's all. Like a lamp.

But Ms. Roberts was the total opposite. She'd been on him from the second he'd zipped up his skull and crossbones hoodie and declared himself the scourge of St. John's County.

The line swung some more as Darla climbed down. More than it should have.

"Something isn't—" Brad's voice was cut off by a shriek, a kraken bellowing from the froth below.

As soon as Darla dropped over the ledge, the knot securing the line slipped loose. Nothing tethered Darla to the cliff side. She was in total free-fall.

Until she stopped suddenly, and her body jerked from the sudden stop. But she only stopped for a second, and then she slid at a slower pace, as if in a controlled fall.

Ms. Roberts yelled from above, her voice tight with urgency: "Grab her! I can't hold on much longer!"

Brad and Major North, the tallest among the group, both leaned out of the cave as far as they could to reach for the rope. Neither could.

"Hurry!" Ms. Roberts yelled. "I'm clipped to the line, but she's pulling me over!"

Carter could see the desperation on Brad's face as he stretched beyond comfort, to the point where his arm looked like it might separate at the shoulder.

And then...

Darla was gone.

Time slowed. Darla dropped out of sight. Ms. Roberts screamed from above as she was dragged over the edge, mother and daughter now both plummeting toward certain death. There was a split second of abject hopelessness as Carter and crew watched their comrades rushed toward their ends.

But it only lasted a second.

Because in the next second, Brad dove out of the cave. He grabbed the tangle of vines that had snaked around Carter with one hand, and the line that held Darla and her mother with the other. He wrapped his legs around the vines, then wove his arm around it, and waited.

For what felt like forever.

Then Ms. Roberts fell past them.

Carter remembered the look on her face. She didn't look at all like the Ms. Roberts who was terrible to him for as long as he could remember. She looked like a child. A frightened child. Make that a scared-to-death child.

Time sped up again as she passed. There one second, gone the next. Carter watched Brad—waited for the moment the line snapped taught and ripped him off his vine, leaving Carter totally and completely alone.

The line snapped. Brad screamed. But he held on. The rope dug into his arms, like it was trying to hold onto him just as much as he was trying to hold onto it.

Major North dropped onto this belly at the edge of the cliff. "Grab my legs!"

Tim and Kevin each grabbed a leg. The major inched out, half his body hanging over nothing. Then more than half. He started to slip through the cadets' hands.

Carter snapped from his state of shock and rushed forward. "Come on," he ordered his crew. "Let us be damned to the locker if we let two of our own meet their ends like this." He grabbed onto Major North's left leg.

Yvette grabbed his right. Walter grabbed Yvette. Louis wrapped his arms around Kevin's waist, and pulled back. Even Nestor and JJ grabbed hold where they could.

Major North stretched out. "Just…" He brushed the line with the tip of his finger. "A little…" He stretched some more, forcing his arm to reach beyond its capability. "Got it!" He grasped the line in an iron tight-grip. "Pull me back!"

The entire group heaved backward into the cave. Once on solid ground, the major reeled in the line, handing the slack back to whoever would take it. He grabbed Brad by the shoulders and hoisted him in. Then they all pulled together, until Darla and Ms. Roberts were safe.

Everyone collapsed into one big ball of relief.

Ms. Roberts wrapped Darla in a bone-crunching hug.

"You saved my life," Darla said in shock and disbelief.

Ms. Roberts looked her daughter determinedly in the eye. "Just because you don't always like me, doesn't mean that I don't always love you." She wrapped her up again. And then she did something that made Carter think she must have banged her head during her fall.

She gestured for Brad to join them.

Brad looked behind him, making sure she wasn't motioning to someone else.

Ms. Roberts grabbed his arm and pulled him into the biggest group bear hug of his life. When she kissed him on the cheek, Brad looked like he might have a stroke. "For saving my little girl," she said. "Maybe I was wrong about you. Forgive me?"

"Uh, okay." The color had drained completely from his face. "Can I have your permission to—"

"Don't ruin the moment," Ms. Roberts said.

The hug broke up, and Brad could breathe again. Until Major North approached him.

The major looked even larger in the confines of the cave. Brad jumped when the major's hand shot upright. He saluted. "Well done, Humbolt."

The cadets snapped their hands to their foreheads, and all three said in unison, "Valley Forge Military Academy! Hoo-rah!"

As the major dropped his hand and pivoted away from Brad, Carter shot across the cave and buried his face in his brother's chest. "I'm glad you're not dead." His voice was muffled by Brad's body.

When his face grew hot and his eyes threatened mutiny and tears, Carter pushed away and marched further in to the cave. "Enough of the niceties," he barked in his pirate voice. "There's treasure to be had."

24

The further they moved into the cave, the more Carter felt like he was being swallowed. They were just walking down the throat of some giant rock monster, serving themselves up as dinner. The sunlight had long since disappeared, with only the dim flickering light of the lanterns casting an eerie glow remaining. But nothing in the world could make Carter turn back now. No cave monsters could make him abandon his quest for treasure. Not even the blatantly booby-trapped section of floor they'd reached about forty minutes into their trek.

The rock and dirt floor of the cave suddenly changed to a seemingly endless honeycomb pattern of tiles of all shapes, colors, and sizes. Nothing like this was done without purpose. And Carter could think of no other purpose than to protect a mound of gold and jewels.

But not every member of his ever-growing crew had the mind of a pirate. Tim and Kevin charged ahead, excited by the sight of something new. Hoo-rah! Like kids on Christmas morning.

"I wouldn't do that if I were you," Carter said as the cadets ran past.

They stopped and turned on their heels. "Yeah? And why not?" one of them asked. Carter didn't care much about trying to tell the twins apart.

"Booby traps."

The cadets chuckled. Like kids.

"Obviously," Carter said. "You think the pirates just wanted to add some color to their cave? They wanted to redecorate a little?"

The cadets exchanged a look. Carter saw the spite in it. Even if they thought he was right, they were going to charge ahead anyway. And they did.

As soon as Tim, or Kevin (who cares, really?), stepped on the tiles, two of them sunk into the ground, and a low rumbling echoed through the cave.

"What's that noise?" Tim asked, shaking.

In answer to his question, a pair of swivel cannons flipped down from a fissure in the wall, their short fuses lighting as they scraped against the rock, their sizable barrels aimed directly at the spiteful cadets.

Any other captain might have let them suffer the consequences of not heeding his warning. But he was not any other captain. He was Captain Lackbeard, and, like it or not, these two were members of his crew now.

Carter rushed forward. He felt a hand brush over his back. Brad tried to grab him, but couldn't get a grip. Carter saw the fuse burning down out of the corner of his eye. Just seconds left. He dove, shoved the twins to the side, away from the tiles, and then he landed hard on the cave floor.

Unfortunately, Carter didn't move with the force he'd hoped. He pushed the twins out of the way, only to land exactly where they stood—smack dab in the crosshairs of the two swivel guns.

He shut his eyes, like that might make getting blasted to smithereens more tolerable.

Maybe it did. He didn't feel anything. He thought there would at least be a pinch. Maybe a burn. A tickle. Something.

He opened his eyes and looked down the two barrels. Both fuses had burned down completely. But no smithereens.

"Misfire," he said, breathless. He stepped back from the tiles, onto the relative safety of solid rock. Just as he did...

BOOM!

Both swivel guns fired, blasting the spot where he stood a second before into total nothingness.

All color drained from Carter's face, the implications of his messiest near-death experience yet hitting him hard in the chest. "I think I need to change my shorts."

Louis produced his Hello Kitty suitcase, tears of relief streaming down his cheeks. "I've got you covered. Hope you like pink."

When the rest of them moved to embrace Carter, and congratulate him on his bravery and not dying, he shouted, "Nobody move!"

They all froze in place.

"What? What is it? What happened?" Marcus ducked and bobbed, evading an unseen barrage of cannon fire.

"This whole area is booby-trapped."

"How do you know?" Yvette asked.

"It's what I would do," Carter answered.

Yvette pointed at Nestor and JJ. "I vote we make them stroll through the pirate's gauntlet. I'm sure they could locate all the traps for us, being expert pirates and all."

Nestor sneered.

Carter took the old map from his pocket. He studied the front, then the terrain, then the map again. The answer was on there somewhere. It had to be. No pirate would rig his own treasure so that not even he could retrieve it.

But it wouldn't be written plainly for anyone to see. He was missing something. He flipped the map over. The back of the map was covered in a crimson splatter. It looked like a pen exploded on it.

Pirates don't do anything without reason.

He looked closer. Underneath the indistinct smear, he started to notice a pattern—a familiar honeycomb pattern. Holding the map below one of the wall lanterns, Carter studied it more intently. There were marks hidden in the red. Very distinct marks that seemed deliberate. He compared it to the tiled floor again.

A slow smile crept across his face. And then, to satisfy his curiosity, he sniffed the map, and then dabbed the red splatter to his tongue.

"*Dios mio!*" Yvette shouted. "That's disgusting."

"Blood," Carter said.

Yvette wretched. "Yeah, not helping."

"It's genius," Carter said. "The pirate that made this map wrote himself a little reminder right here on how to bypass his traps. As all good pirates do. Only, he must have run out of ink, because this is drawn in blood."

"You probably just contracted syphilis or something," Marcus said.

"Worth it," Carter said.

"I don't think you know what syphilis is," Yvette said.

"Whatever," Carter said. "The point is, I know where the traps are. Now we just need a way to trip them so we can get through." He pointed to the grenade launcher in Major North's hand. "Can you shoot some of them?"

The major shook his head. "I'm out."

"I have one round left," Ms. Roberts said, taking the bean bag shell out of her pocket.

"I don't think one will be enough," Carter said. "Unless..." His voice trailed off following a crazy thought. "Louis, you still have your marbles?"

Louis nodded, but didn't seem to grasp the consequences of that nod until Carter snatched the leather pouch of marbles from him.

Seeming to understand Carter's plan before Carter could explain, Major North began to disassemble the bean bag cartridge. When he was done, he'd separated the bean bag from its casing.

Carter handed him the pouch of marbles.

"I got those when I was six," Louis said, his head on Yvette's shoulder as she reluctantly consoled him. "They've been with me through thick and thin."

"Well, kid," the major said, emptying the marbles into the casing. "Now they're going to get us all out of the thick of this situation." He secured the casing and examined it to make sure it was secure. Then he loaded it into the grenade launcher.

"You really think this will work?" Major North asked Carter.

Carter shrugged. "When in doubt, blow something up."

The major smiled for the first time that Carter could remember. "I like the way you think." He snapped his hand to his forehead in salute.

Shocked, Carter clumsily returned the gesture.

"You saved my cadets' lives," the major said as he presented Carter with the grenade launcher. "I think you should do the honors."

Every moment in his life, from the second he was born, had been building to this—the moment he fired his first grenade launcher.

Brad didn't seem to think it was as awesome an idea as Carter did. "I have serious concerns about my little brother firing a grenade launcher."

"And I had serious concerns about my big brother jumping off a cliff," Carter said.

"Fair enough," Brad said.

Carter continued before Brad could. "Besides, it's not technically a grenade launcher if it isn't launching grenades. It's just a marble launcher. The coolest, most amazing marble launcher in the universe."

He took aim—high for maximum carnage. "Fire in the hole!"

The marble-filled bean bag burst like an oversized shotgun shell, scattering little glass beads of mayhem throughout the tiled area of the cave. They dug into the rock wall, ricocheted, spread marble-y destruction, and triggered a swath of diabolical pirate traps.

Boarding axes swung out of the walls. Cutlasses windmilled through the air. Muskets, flintlocks, and swivel guns blasted from hidden cracks and crevices.

Carter had unleashed hell. And he loved it.

A thick fog of black smoke and rock dust filled the cave. It clogged the crew's lungs, and they hacked and coughed it back up. Once it cleared, they stood in stunned silence, gazing upon the war zone in front of them.

"Awesome," Carter said, but he couldn't hear himself—his ears were still ringing.

"My poor marbles," Louis sobbed.

"Way to take one for the crew," Marcus said, clapping Louis on the shoulder.

"Follow me," Carter ordered his crew. "Step exactly where I step. I can't be sure that all the traps have been triggered. Wouldn't want anyone getting diced in half or blown into little tiny bits."

"Way to inspire confidence, Captain," Darla said.

"I do what I can," Carter said with a smile.

"Onward!" Walter shouted. "I smell treasure."

"I think that's just mold and mildew," Louis corrected. "But I like the vibe."

Carter blazed the trail, hopscotching and funky-stepping across the tiles, stopping occasionally to consult his blood map. He reached the other side intact, and, even though his legs were screaming for a rest, and the rest of the crew had yet to cross, he couldn't wait. He knew what was around that corner just ahead. He could hear it calling to him.

He ran ahead, turned the corner, and skidded to a halt.

M. G.

Carter wanted to cry, but he knew that was unbecoming of a pirate captain, even one that was just eleven years old.

He basked in the glow of it. Like lying on the beach. He closed his eyes for a moment, took a second to be alone with it.

A sea of treasure.

25

adre de dios." Yvette crossed her herself as she uttered the blessing.

The rest of the crew shared the sentiment. "Valley Forge Military Academy! Hoo-rah!"

In their own way.

The cadets ran into the room and dove into a pile of gold and jewels. They threw gems at each other like they were having a snowball fight.

Louis scooped up a handful of pearls and gazed at them, astonishment adding a glow to his cheeks. "I suppose these will serve as sufficient replacements for my marbles."

Marcus and Yvette walked from pile to pile, admiring the jewelry, the gold, getting lost in the shimmer and shine of it all. Their eyes sparkled as if diamonds had replaced their retinas.

JJ and Nestor threw handfuls of doubloons into the air and let them shower down on them.

Major North caressed the ivory handle of a flintlock pistol, a truly pristine piece of weaponry.

Walter cast his line and brought back a silver crown,

which he promptly set on his head. "King of the sea," he said to himself.

A sparkle caught Brad's eye. He stooped down to pick it up—a diamond ring. Talk about a sign from above. "This might fit your finger," he said to Darla, still down on one knee. "Someday." He flashed her a mischievous smile, but Carter saw the honesty in it. Now Brad could have his wish. A house. A family.

A normal life.

Carter turned away from them, his crew, his friends, his...whatever the old folks were. They all had their dreams, their plans, but he still didn't know what his were. He didn't know exactly what he wanted.

He wanted adventure, and he got it. It was done. He had his treasure. But what was he going to do with it? Have a normal life? He didn't even know what that meant. All he knew was the orphanage, his friends, his brother.

And all that was ending.

He walked along the edge of the cavern, so many sparkly things that his eyes just skipped along, not focusing on one or the other. Until they spotted a gap in the sparkle—a waist-high hole in the cavern wall.

He squatted down, and crawled through.

The light from the cavern only reached a few feet into this tunnel. Carter turned on his headlamp only to have the light flicker and dim. The battery was dying. He crawled faster, hoping to reach the end before it died completely.

The raucous celebration faded behind him as a new sound grew ahead of him—something like a roar, a rumble. The ceiling of the tunnel vanished, and Carter knew he'd reached the end. He stood and, with the last flicker of light from his lamp, he saw another lantern mounted on the wall. He opened his box of matches and felt around inside.

One match left. Fitting. The end of the journey. The final match. He struck it, and lit the lantern. Like the others, this lantern set off a chain reaction, a cannon fuse sparking and lighting several more mounted along the wall. Except here, the fuse ran horizontal and vertical. The one Carter lit was only one in the first row. There were at least a dozen rows climbing several stories high.

Carter followed the trail of sparks as it climbed all the way to the top. It looked like the night sky, full of stars.

As his eyes fell, they didn't land on the sea of treasure that made the chest in the other room look like a small piggy bank, or any one of the dozen chests that looked to be vomiting riches. No, his eyes landed on something else.

The throne.

A high-backed, gilded chair, arms upholstered in velvet, intricate designs that reminded Carter of waves carved into its legs. Truly fit for a king. Perhaps that is who the man sitting on it was—a king. Back when he had muscles and skin and a face and brains, before he had rotted to a wealthy skeleton.

Carter stepped softly, walked quietly toward the skeleton. He imagined its eyes following him, and felt the sudden urge to say something. "Hi, I'm Carter. I mean, Captain Lackbeard."

No response. Obviously.

Carter reminded himself that the skeleton was dead. There was absolutely no way that Carter was about to awaken an undead pirate king, who would then lead his undead pirate crew on a campaign to conquer the seas and spread un-death to the four corners of the world.

No way.

"I found your map," Carter said. "Stole it, actually," he added with some pride. "Because I'm a pirate. That's what we do. You understand." Carter laughed uncomfortably to himself.

He was just out of arm's reach of the skeleton now, but oddly, being that close helped to ease Carter's fears. He saw then that it was no demon, just bones in nice clothing.

Sadness washed over Carter. Unexpected, he didn't know why or what to do with it, which just made him angry. Then, tired and confused, he sat on the floor at the dead pirate king's feet.

He looked up at the skeleton and realized why he was so sad.

This pirate king, a lord of the sea, sitting on his golden throne in a sea of treasure. This is what Carter wanted to be. The dream he had.

But now, looking at the fancy skeleton, Carter saw that the pirate king was just alone. He had his adventure, his riches, but where was his crew? What was a pirate without his crew?

"He's nothing," Carter said, staring into the pirate king's empty eye sockets. "Nothing."

"Carter?" Brad's voice echoed in the small tunnel connecting the two caverns.

Carter stood at the mouth of the tunnel and shouted back. Moments later, Brad and the rest of the crew emerged, and Carter delighted at the looks of shock and amazement on their faces.

"We did it," Carter said wrapping his arms around one and then another. "The greatest adventure. We are pirates." He looked at Brad. "Now let's go home." Carter watched the shock on his brother's face turn to confusion, and then a content smile.

Brad slapped his hand down on Carter's shoulder. "Aye aye, Captain."

"Question," Louis said, raising his hand. "How are we supposed to get all this treasure to the boat?"

Carter gestured to the pirate king, and smiled. "Pirates never do anything without a plan." He motioned for the crew to follow as he walked around behind the throne. A large portrait of a fancy-looking gentleman, like an English nobleman or something, rested against the cavern wall. He slid it to the side to reveal an opening.

He and Brad stuck their heads in. A platform, about five feet by five feet, hung from the rock ceiling by a rope that was attached to a pulley system. The platform could lower all the way to the water, forty feet below, where their boat would be waiting.

"That must be how he got all this so far inland by himself," Carter said.

"How do you know he was by himself?" Brad asked.

Carter spread his arms wide, gesturing to the sea of treasure, and then to the pirate king. "All this, and just him. He obviously didn't share any with his crew. He just sat there and looked at it. Didn't use it for more adventures or a comfortable life in some big house. He just sat on his throne, all by himself, in a dark cave."

Brad clapped his brother on the back. "He didn't have a pirate's soul. He had a greedy soul."

Carter nodded. "Let's get this stuff loaded up. I want off this island and back on the sea."

The crew shouted in unison. "Aye aye!"

They split into teams, each with different tasks. Walter, Darla, and Yvette hiked back to get the ship. Nestor, JJ, Marcus, Brad, and Major North lugged the treasure from the smaller cavern into the larger, and then moved all the treasure to the lift. Carter, Louis, Ms. Roberts, and the cadets loaded the lift, and lowered it down once the boat arrived.

The cavern was empty of gold and silver and jewels surprisingly fast. Two by two, the crew took the lift down to the treasure-laden deck of the ship, until only Brad and Carter remained.

Carter took one last minute to study the pirate king, alone on his throne.

"Ready?" Brad asked.

"What's going to happen once we get back?"

"Don't know. Divide up the treasure. Probably bribe the boat owners so they don't press charges."

"No," Carter said. "I mean, with us. Are you and Darla going to get married? Buy a big house with a yard and a swing set and have kids and barbecues and the newspaper delivered to your front step?"

"No one reads the newspaper anymore," Brad said.

Carter punched him in the arm, but there was no oomph behind it. "You know what I mean."

Brad threw up his arms. "I don't know, Carter. What do you want me to say? That none of those things will ever happen? I can't, because, you never know. They might. But not anytime soon. I mean, I'll go to college first—"

"Yeah, and what's the difference? You're still going somewhere I can't follow. And where does that leave me?" He pointed at the pirate captain. "It leaves me just like this guy."

Brad walked away from Carter, his shoulders heaving, like he was trying to keep calm. But when he came back, his eyes looked a little red and misty. "You probably don't remember this—I think you were too young—but Mom took us to a pirate museum when we were little. She went into the hospital the next week. And she never came out. That was the last time the three of us did something together."

The memory flashed in Carter's head.

"Mom bought you that pirate teddy bear that you had forever," Brad said. "But she bought me something, too." He reached into his back pocket and pulled out a keychain—a pair of crossed swords.

It looked like a cheap thing, plastic, your typical gift shop fare that could be broken with a mild tug. But Carter saw the importance of the thing in Brad's eyes.

"Mom knew she was sick," Brad said. "She told me that when sailors turned pirate, they swore an oath, sometimes on a sword. So she bought me this, and made me swear an oath. That I would always look out for you. Always."

The world got wavy as the tears built in Carter's eyes. Then his cheeks got hot, and he felt like a total jerk. All the times he wished Brad would leave him alone or lighten up or stop being such a drag. All the times he got angry at Brad for not taking this adventure seriously.

Brad was the real pirate. The real captain.

Brad tucked the keychain back into his pocket. "What happens to a pirate who breaks his oath?" Brad cleared his throat, and then spoke with harsh pirate's voice. "He shall be met with a death most swift and painful."

Carter laughed and the tears spilled down his cheek. Brad clapped his brother on the shoulder. "Let's go, Captain. Our adventure isn't done yet."

26

Phyllis Katzenbacher, heiress to the largest marshmallow fortune in the world, sipped tea and considered how lives change—both hers and that of the strange child sitting across from her.

The tea room, once a benign taupe shade, something in the coffee range, was now a brilliant vermillion, speckled with eggplant polka-dots. It looked like the eggshell of an exotic bird, or perhaps a dinosaur.

Phyllis then imagined that she was inside the dinosaur egg. She would be a raptor, most definitely. Something fierce and feared, but still graceful.

She ordered it painted on the way home and, by the time she stepped foot inside her absurdly large and luxurious mansion, it was as she desired. When you are as disgustingly wealthy as the glamorous Phyllis Katzenbacher, all things are as you desire.

Well, most things.

This child, for example. It was not the one she'd chosen from the catalogue. She'd ordered a boy. Someone with a sturdy back. Jeeves wasn't getting any younger, and she would one day need a replacement for him. But this child had tricked her. She did not enjoy being tricked.

Phyllis looked over the rim of her china teacup, which was laced with gold, at Linn, as it called itself, staring off as if at nothing. She was an odd child. Not like any other she had encountered. Though, to be fair, she had encountered very few.

Phyllis Katzenbacher never had children of her own. She never particularly wanted children, but she never particularly didn't want children, either. She figured she would get around to it eventually, but she simply forgot. She spent her younger days globetrotting and rubbing elbows with the richest elbows in the world, some royal elbows, even. She had seen more adventure in her life than Indiana Jones and Lara Croft rolled into one. And, yes, she knew who Lara Croft was. Her tastes were wide-ranging.

Who thinks of children while exploring shipwrecks in the Bermuda Triangle, or learning to paint with the masters in Paris? But her adventures had slowed as of late. Reluctantly, because her body had slowed, but not her mind. And so, her active mind wandered to children. Or, perhaps, he heart did. As often as she told herself that she only needed a younger model of Jeeves, she knew that her extravagant house felt most empty these days. Jeeves was like a butler ghost, appearing when she required his services and then fading into the ether like a gust of wind when his services were rendered. Aside from him, it was just her.

But not anymore.

"What are you thinking of, child?" she asked Linn.

Linn sipped her tea as she scanned the walls. "I was just imagining that I was a dinosaur."

Phyllis smiled.

Just then, Jeeves materialized beside her. He whispered in her ear and handed her a manila envelope. Then he vanished back to wherever stealthy butlers go. Were there hidden passages in the walls? Phyllis would need to consult the original blueprints.

Phyllis removed the contents of the envelope, a series of satellite images, and studied them carefully. She leaned back in her chair and tapped her chin with a long, crooked finger. She thought for a while about whether she should share this information with Linn. It would surely drive her to act. But would it drive her back to her old life? Away from sipping tea in a dinosaur egg?

A surge of adrenaline suddenly rushed through Phyllis's veins with the onset of an idea. An adventure. It had been so long. Maybe the time of adventuring had not passed. Maybe she just needed someone to share them with.

"It seems your friends are in somewhat of a pickle," Phyllis said, testing the waters. "I imagine it is in some way related to how you came to be sitting in my tea room rather than the young man I meant to retrieve."

Linn leaned forward, worry crinkling her nose. "What happened?"

Phyllis handed her the photos. Aerial photographs of a marina. Several kids steering a sailboat.

Linn looked up from the photos. "How did you get these?"

Phyllis smiled. "Inquisitive. I adore that. Some people have satellite TV. We have satellites."

"We?" Linn asked.

Phyllis gestured toward the room with a grand

sweeping motion. "You are a Katzenbacher now, dear. What's mine is yours."

Linn set down her tea, stood from her chair, and paced the inside of the dinosaur egg. Phyllis could feel the concern radiating from the girl. She took a final sip of her tea before setting it down. She leaned back in her chair and folded her hands on her lap.

"I do not have many people in this world I would consider a friend," Phyllis said. "Like a family, I never took the time to make them. But I do know this."

Linn stopped pacing when she circled around and stood in front of Phyllis.

The old woman stood, with some effort, and put her hand on Linn's shoulder. "If you have a friend in need, then you do whatever you are capable of doing to help them."

"But they've set sail," Linn said. "Without me. I don't know where they are."

Phyllis motioned toward the stack of satellite photos. "Clearly, we have the means to locate them."

"But we would still need to reach them. Do you have a boat?"

The weight of Phyllis's frown pulled her head to one side.

"Do *we* have a boat?" Linn corrected herself.

Phyllis smiled, and her head righted itself. "We do, indeed."

27

The deck of the ship was conspicuously closer to the surface of the ocean than the last time Carter stepped foot on it, but for good reason. Weighted down with treasure. The best reason there ever could be.

They would need to take it slow on the way home. The last thing he wanted was to capsize and lose all his hard-won treasure just before the finish line. And also dying. Dying just before the finish line was also bad. *Really* bad. But he had faith in his ship, in his crew, in everything.

At that moment, life was everything that he had ever wanted it to be.

Eleuthera behind them. Home and glory ahead of them.

"Avast ye!" Carter yelled from atop of chest full of treasure. "Crew, come to order."

Some of the newcomers grumbled at having orders barked at them, but they begrudgingly obliged. Which was good, because it was the newcomers, specifically, who Carter was addressing.

"To share in the plunder, ye need to go on account." He held the Hello Kitty journal high.

"On account of what?" Tim asked.

Carter and Major North both sighed. "You have to become pirates," Carter said.

"Cool," Tim said. "I'm down."

Both cadets rushed forward and signed their names with vigor. Then they hopped around the deck practicing their "ayes" and "me hardies".

Major North wasn't quite so excited. "I'm not used to taking orders. How 'bout I become captain?"

Carter crossed his arms. "How 'bout you fly your helicopter home?"

"First Mate?" the major countered.

"That position is currently occupied," Carter said. "Unless he wishes to step aside?"

"Not a chance," Brad said.

"Quartermaster?" the major said. "I know a thing or two about weapons."

Carter tapped his chin. After a moment of thought, he said, "Deal."

Major North smiled, and signed.

Walter stepped forward, shoving past the major and yanking the pen from his hand. "Give it here, biceps." He leaned over the book, close to Carter. His eyes took on an ominous shine. "There's a shark wandering these waters whom I mean to have words with. I join your crew, you help me settle old scores?"

"Join my crew, and your scores are my scores."

Walter nodded and smiled, and added his name.

Ms. Roberts stepped forward. She eyed Carter the way she always did—like he was a newly discovered species of lizard, one that could be poisonous, could be friendly, could transform into Godzilla. She was always on guard around him, and he never understood why.

"You know why I came after you?" she asked Carter.

He suddenly felt like he should be tip-toeing. "To get Darla?"

Ms. Roberts didn't seem to expect that answer. "Right, of course. Absolutely." She turned to her daughter. "Love you, sweetie."

Darla shook her head.

"But, also, I came after you for the same reason you left—adventure." She leaned back and crossed her arms the way she did when she caught Carter sneaking into the kitchen after curfew. "You never pictured me doing anything outside the orphanage, did you?"

Carter shook his head.

Ms. Roberts sighed, and her arms unfolded. "I was hard on you. I know that. But it's because I saw a lot of myself in you. I used to crave adventure. I used to be wild. Seeing you, still wild, maybe I got jealous."

For the first time in, well, forever, Carter saw Ms. Roberts in a different light. He handed her the pen. "You need to sign this. I think you've got a pirate's soul."

She took it, pretended to have something in her eye, and signed.

Carter extended the pen to JJ and Nestor, the only two yet to sign. "We may have gotten off on the wrong foot, but you came around. Make your mark. Be one of us."

They looked at each other, hesitation in their eyes.

"No signature, no share."

The hesitation left their eyes. Only to be replaced with malice.

"Why take a share, when we can take it all?" Nestor

said. He and JJ each pulled a pair of flintlock pistols from under their shirts.

Carter threw his hands up. "Seriously? We were having a moment."

"Consider it your last moment," JJ said. "Now, walk." He shoved Carter toward the bow.

"I thought you turned over a new leaf," Carter said.

"We're pirates," Nestor said. "On a boat full of treasure. What did you expect? This is what pirates do."

Carter turned around to face them. "Only if you want to end up like the pirate king—alone, rich, and dead. A pirate is nothing without his crew. They're his family."

Something caught his eye then, behind the scoundrel turncoats, zooming toward them from the horizon. "And they always surprise you."

"There won't be any surprises this time, kid," Nestor said.

Carter grinned. No surprises, huh?

Speeding toward them was a 200-foot-long luxury yacht complete with three decks and a helipad. Standing on the bow, in matching nautically-themed outfits of yellow and red polka dots and derby hats that inexplicably managed to stay on their heads, was Phyllis and Linn Katzenbacher.

Only the best surprise ever!

The yacht pulled up beside them so that Phyllis and Linn stood just feet from Nestor and JJ.

"You were saying?" Carter said to Nestor.

"Who are you supposed to be?" Nestor said. "Aside from our next victim."

Phyllis planted her foot on the railing of her ship and dug her fists into her hips—a pirate captain's pose if ever there was one. "The cavalry. Now, put down your weapons and nobody gets hurt."

JJ's flintlock pistol shook as he laughed. "Seeing how you've clearly been around a while, I figured you'd know this. First rule of life, as previously explained—those with the weapons make the rules."

Phyllis and Linn erupted in a chipmunk-like cackle. "Very true," Phyllis said. "Second rule of life—don't try to intimidate someone captaining a 150-million-dollar yacht with a couple rusty pistols you found in a cave."

The deck of the yacht suddenly swarmed with an army of heavily armed mercenaries moonlighting as private security officers, all wearing body armor and carrying high-tech assault rifles.

The flintlock pistols clattered on the deck, sounding JJ and Nestor's surrender.

"You stepped in what?" Carter said to Nestor and JJ.

Brad and Darla tossed a line to the officers on the luxury yacht, who then pulled the ships closer. The officers jumped over and secured the traitorous swine. They didn't heed Carter's suggestion to toss the scum to the sharks, but tied and gagged them and dragged them below deck instead.

Several rounds of cheers rolled over the deck. The excitement nearly swept Carter overboard. He didn't even notice Linn until she was standing right in front of him. The noise around him died away, drowned out by the noise of Linn's outfit.

"I missed you," she said.

Carter said nothing.

"I thought I'd never see you again," she continued.

Again, he said nothing.

The deep red that rose in her cheeks complemented her ensemble. "Aren't you going to say anything?"

The desire to speak the perfect words choked Carter so that he could say nothing. Then he cleared his throat, and Captain Lackbeard spoke. "When faced with the prospect of life, there is only one action worth taking."

In one smooth motion—the smoothest motion that Carter had ever made, maybe the smoothest motion he would ever make—he took Linn in his arms and planted a kiss on her.

When he pulled away, they both looked like they'd seen ghosts in the other's eyes. But smiles slowly spread over their white faces as the shock wore off and cheers of "hip-hip hooray!" sounded all around them.

28

Cameras flashed like cannon fire as the ship docked at the Camachee Island Marina. News crews hollered questions that bled into each other and ended up sounding like a blob of noise.

Photographers scaled neighboring boats and climbed on the roof of the marina office to get pictures of the treasure-laden ship of Captain Lackbeard and his crew. Reporters crowded the dock hoping for an interview.

But there were only two people Carter cared to speak with. Two people he was indebted to, and a true pirate always paid his debts.

The two owners of the ship that Carter and company had commandeered pushed their way through the mob, toward the ship.

"Now, listen here, you rapscallion," the old man said. "How dare you abscond with our boat! That boat is like a member of the family. Like our child. And you took it from us. And to leave an IOU? How insulting." He waved the scrap of paper that Carter left tacked to the dock when they took the boat.

"Sir, ma'am." Carter stood like a captain, feet

shoulder-width apart, hands behind his back, chin up. "I took what's yours, I don't deny that. Your ship has served us well. She took us across the sea, stood against attacking pirates, and brought us home safe."

The man opened his mouth to yell at Carter again, but Carter cut him off.

"She brought us and our considerable treasure home again."

The boat-owners' eyes sparkled like jewels.

Carter took another scrap of paper from his pocket. On it was written an amount that he and the crew had already agreed upon. An amount he never imagined he would ever write down, let alone have the ability to give away. He handed the paper to the man.

"And here is your just compensation—if we can keep the ship."

The man objected, refusing to take the paper. "Now, see here, you can't just—"

The woman snatched the paper. Her eyes bulged as she read it. "Sonny, you got yourself a boat." She pulled her husband away before he could argue further, shoving the paper in his face and telling him to quiet down.

Before Carter could inform his crew of the good news, the sea of reporters parted, and a man in a finely tailored suit passed through.

"What did I tell you?" the man said to Carter, his voice sharp with accusation. "I said to embrace your pirate soul, but *never* at my expense."

"But, Mr. Croce—"

"You found a treasure map in an artifact belonging to me. Last I checked, that's stealing." He stared holes in Carter. "Well? Anything to say?"

"According to Blackbeard, the greatest pirate ever to sail the seven seas..." Carter cleared his throat, and adopted his pirate's brogue. "Stealing is just a landlubber's term for the appropriation of goods that shoulda belonged to me in the first place."

Croce's face went blank.

"At sea, possession is ten-tenths of the law," Carter continued. He pointed to the ship, lousy with treasure. "*That* is possession, and *I* am the law."

Croce's face was stone. His eyes were cold and black. And then he laughed. "Well played, kid."

A new round of cheers erupted from the crew, and like a tidal wave, it washed over the gathered crowd of reporters and onlookers. It was infectious, the sense of adventure accomplished, of victory, of camaraderie.

Croce leaned in close, so he could speak to Carter through the noise. "Of course, I will be displaying some of that treasure in my museum."

"Of course," Carter said. "Assuming your terms meet my approval."

"Don't push it, kid."

Carter rejoined his crew on the deck of the ship and faced the reporters. He raised his hands, calling for them to quiet.

They didn't quiet fast enough for Marcus's liking. "Captain Lackbeard will now make a statement," he shouted.

When there was pin-drop silence, Carter cleared his throat. "There is an old saying," Carter began. "That he who dies with the most toys wins. But I say, he who *lives* with the most treasure wins." He looked from one side to the other. Flanked by his crew. His family. "But you don't need a map or a boat to find the greatest treasure." His eyes fell on Linn. "That's because you've had it all along."

THE END

Acknowledgments

The hardiest of thanks to Adam Rocke for continuing to find me a fit writing partner. And to the entire team at Common Deer Press for all of their tireless work and dedication. And to Molly, my wife and partner, without whom I would accomplish nothing.

-CS

I'd like to thank Pat Croce, who schooled me on the realm of pirates and the Golden Age of Piracy. If ever there was a man with a pirate's soul, it's you.

-AR

About

CODY grew up and continues to grow up in the Adirondacks. He hunts for mythical creatures amongst the pines with his two sons and his cat. His wife leads the expeditions. He writes books and comics and to-do lists and occasionally crosses items off said lists, but mostly just doodles on them.

ADAM has dived for pirate treasure in the Caribbean, dug for ancient artifacts in Europe, hunted for poachers in Africa, played poker with cartel kingpins in Juarez, scouted for UFOs in the Sonora Desert, raced in both the Baja 1000 and The Gumball Rally, swam with great white sharks sans cage, jumped out of a plane sans parachute, cave-dived sans sanity and, courtesy of a secondary degree in Cryptozoology, taken part in Sasquatch safaris and other "crypto-quests" around the world.